Chimera

A Kate Redman Mystery: Book 5

Celina Grace

Prologue

THE NIGHT SKY OVER ABBEYFORD was spangled with a million little explosions of light; red, blue, gold and green lit up the dark clouds before falling and fading into oblivion. In the town below, the crowds thronged the pavements and the open space of the fairground that lay to the north of the town park gardens. Along the high street came a fantastic beast, jointed in three places; a giant, scaled snake with huge yellow eyes. Children yelled and pointed, and adults clapped and cheered at the sight. Beneath the snake costume, fifteen sweating men held up the frame that supported its body. The night air carried the acrid tang of cordite from the fireworks and billowed with smoke from chestnuts cooking on braziers. It was thick with the greasy smell of the fast food vans offering chips and hot dogs and candy floss. Thumping bass music blared from the funfair on the park ground itself, pierced by the shrieks and delighted yells of those on the fast rides and the bumper cars. Abbeyford was enjoying its annual pagan festival; for one night in late September the town celebrated the myth and legend of the Abbeyford Wyrm, a giant snake-like creature once rumoured to have lived in the woods and forests surrounding the town.

Olly Chandler had something more than the festival on his mind. He and his girlfriend, Mia Smith, strolled through the fairground, hand in hand. Mia wanted to go on the Ghost Train but Olly scoffed. "Got something even better than that," he said, pulling Mia close. "A quiet place just for us and some decent weed. How about that?"

Mia looked at him, pouting. Then she giggled. "Let's get stoned and *then* go on the Ghost Train," she said, close to his ear. Her warm breath and the way she licked his neck after she spoke made him even more anxious to get her to where they were going.

"Come on," he said and pulled at her hand. They ran, Mia a little awkwardly in her high heels, over the dusty, bruised grass of the park towards the dip of the hill and the river beyond it.

"Where we going, Olly?" Mia asked as they left the lighter area of the park and walked into the darkness, relieved only here and there by dim streetlights.

"You'll see. We used to go there when we were kids. It's private – no one ever goes there."

"Okay." She sounded doubtful. Olly found the

footpath somehow – it was much more overgrown that it used to be – and pushed aside tree branches and brambles.

"Down there?" said Mia. She actually sounded nervous now. "What is it?"

"S'alright," said Olly, conscious of a little spike of uneasiness himself. "It's a row of little houses. They're empty now, been like that for years." The two of them pushed through the last of the undergrowth and came out onto a little back road. There were no lights but the moon had emerged from behind a cloud and cast a silvery radiance over the tumbledown buildings before them.

"Are you sure this is safe?" Mia looked down at herself, strewn with leaves and bits of undergrowth, and tutted. "Look at my top. This had better be worth it."

"It's fine," Olly said impatiently. The desire he'd felt at the fairground was ebbing away, down here in the darkness and silence, not to mention the faint unpleasant smell that hung in the air. Maybe this wasn't such a good idea after all. But where else did they have to go? He thought resentfully of his older brother, who'd recently gained his driving license. Only another year to go before Olly could take his test. He couldn't wait.

Mia was still hanging back, and Olly felt protective. He pulled her close to him and kissed her, and she responded enthusiastically. "Come on, it'll be fine," he said. "You want to, don't you?"

"'Course." Mia took his hand trustingly and he led her through a space in the front garden wall of the first house in the row of three, where a gate had once hung.

Olly chose the first house because it was the nearest. If he remembered rightly, the door looked closed but could be opened with a shove. Though the house on the end had no front door at all… perhaps they should go there? No, they wanted a bit of privacy. Definitely this one, Olly thought to himself, a decision that would prove to cost him years of therapy.

They stumbled up the garden path to the front door, black in the moonlight. Olly put a hand out to the peeling paint and gave it a shove. The door creaked open and he felt a quick moment of triumph before the smell hit them in the face.

"Ugh, ugh, that's *disgusting*," shrieked Mia. "I'm not going in *there*."

"It's okay, it's going, it's going." A night breeze whipped up and carried the worst of the stench away. "Come on," said Olly, desperately. He couldn't have said himself why he was so hell bent on getting into the cottage now, though his family would have told him it was because he had a stubborn streak a mile wide running through him.

He almost dragged Mia into the darkness of the

cottage. Once inside, the smell returned and Olly almost gagged. Mia made a small, choked noise behind him. The inside of the cottage was pitch black, so black that as Olly inched forward, fumbling for his phone in order to use its pale screen light as a torch; his feet collided with something hard and he tripped and fell.

His phone went flying and he put both hands out to break his fall. Both hands connected with something that, while ostensibly solid, broke open under the impact of his body. Olly felt his hands sink into something peculiarly liquid and the smell, which had already been terrible enough, intensified to something so repulsive it felt almost like a physical force.

Behind him, Mia held her phone aloft and it cast a pale, ghostly light over the room, showing Olly what he'd actually fallen into. Mia began to scream, but he hardly heard her because, by that time, he was screaming himself.

Chapter One

"THIS IS FREAKIN' AMAZING!" JAY shouted in Kate's ear. "I can't believe you've lived here for four years and never *once* been to this festival."

"I know, I know." Kate was thinking the same thing herself. She'd never seen the normally fairly quiet streets of Abbeyford so busy, packed with a shouting, laughing, gesticulating crowd; from tiny babies in prams to pensioners gamely tottering on their walking sticks or regarding the festivities from wheelchairs. "I always thought it was – well – a bit – a bit..."

"A bit what?" asked Hannah, Kate's best friend who was visiting from Brighton. Hannah's husband, Dan, was standing with his hands in his jeans pockets, a bemused expression on his face. Kate knew how he felt.

"I don't know. A bit...fuddy duddy. Like Morris dancing and the W.I."

"Jesus," said Jay, grinning. "I would have thought something like the Women's Institute was right up your street. You're hardly rock and roll, are you, sis?"

Kate slapped his arm. "Compared to you, no. But then compared to you, the most debauched of the Roman emperors aren't very rock and roll."

That wasn't actually very fair, as she knew full well that Jay had calmed down a lot over the last few years. But he was her little brother - teasing was her prerogative.

The main reason for Jay's newfound sense of responsibility came up and linked her arm with his. "He's like a toddler," said Laura Murray, Jay's girlfriend of the last two years. "He gets overexcited, especially if he's had sugar. I knew that candy floss was a bad idea."

Jay growled and bent his girlfriend over in a backwards wrestling hold. She shrieked and flailed at him until he pulled her back upright, the two of them giggling.

"Come on," said Hannah. "Let's go and get a drink."

"Yes," said Dan in a fervent tone. "All these giant worm things are weirding me out."

They wandered along the crowded streets in a loose group, one or the other of the couples straggling behind or moving ahead. Kate tried not to mind that she was the only single person amongst them.

"There's a really nice pub down by the river,"

said Jay. "Let's head there. It's off the main drag so we'll ditch the crowds, at least."

"Sound good to me," said Kate. "The Boathouse, right?"

"Yep. We need to take the first right up here and go past the fairground."

The fairground was still heaving with people, showing no signs of slowing down for the night. The air was thick with the greasy smell of fried food, with the odd waft of sweetness from the clouds of candy floss being whirled into existence through the machine.

Kate found herself walking next to Hannah. Dan was up ahead, talking football with Jay. "How are you doing?" asked Hannah, linking her arm with Kate's. "I was so sorry to hear about Andrew."

"Oh, that's fine," said Kate, a little uncomfortably. "We just weren't right for one another, that's all."

"But he was lovely!"

"I know," said Kate, "But he wasn't my kind of lovely. Anyway, I'm fine. Don't worry about me. How's my beautiful godson?"

"He's fine. But insane in the way only a two year old can be. He's developed a scream that the army could use as a sonic weapon and he deploys it whenever he doesn't get his own way."

Kate laughed. Hannah always did have a way of putting things. "I must come down and see you soon."

Hannah gave her arm a squeeze. "Yes, do. A few days at the seaside...it'll do you good."

"Mmm." Kate always forgot that to almost everyone else, Brighton was a nice, hip, seaside town. To her, it was one of the hunting grounds of the person who'd almost killed her. She felt her hand moving towards the scar on her back, as it did every time she started thinking about it, and consciously stopped it. Hannah, who must have felt her flinch a little, gave her a quick glance but said nothing, giving her arm another quick, friendly squeeze.

"How's gorgeous Mark?" asked Hannah, after a short silence.

"He's fine, as far as I know. I haven't seen him for a few weeks – he and Jeff have been living it up in the Caribbean for a fortnight."

"Coo, nice. All right for some."

"He deserves it. He works hard. Mind you," Kate paused, considering, "so do I."

"Your Inspector exams are coming up, aren't they? Are you nervous?"

Kate shrugged. "A bit. I've been revising like hell, though. It's just...I don't know what to anticipate, really. It's been ages since I've done any kind of written exam."

"Well," said Hannah comfortably. "I'm sure you'll be fine. You always did better than me at college, that's for sure."

They walked on. The lights and noise of the

fairground retreated a little as they moved away from the main part of the town park gardens and onto the wide footpath that led down the river and the footbridge that crossed it. Stately iron lamp posts, a nod to the park's Victorian heritage, stood at intervals along the footpath, casting a faint orange glow over the group as they made their way down the gentle slope of the hill.

Hannah and Kate had outpaced the others by about fifty feet, Kate's usual fast walking pace having swept her friend along. They had almost reached flat ground down by the banks of the river, and the iron railings that spanned the footbridge could dimly be seen up ahead in the street lights.

"Jay's grown up a lot, hasn't he?" Hannah said quietly as they walked along.

Kate looked at her in surprise. She'd noticed that about her little brother but it was heartening to see that someone else had too. Mind you, Hannah had known her and Jay since they were fourteen and five respectively; she was almost as close as family. Come to think of it, Kate thought, remembering several family members, Hannah was closer.

"He has," she agreed. "It's Laura's influence, I think. God, I hope they never split up."

Hannah smiled. "Well, they might not. They might even get married, one day."

The thought gave Kate a jolt. She smiled to hide the small tremor that Hannah's remark had given her. She didn't want Jay to get married before her. I'm much older than him. It should be me first. But...fat chance of that happening anytime soon.

Hannah was saying something else but Kate held up a hand to stop her, frowning.

"What is it?" Hannah asked.

"I'm not sure – shush for a moment. I thought I heard something..."

They both listened. For a moment, there was nothing, just the busy silence of the landscape around them and then the wind changed and they both heard it – the faint sound of screaming.

"Wait here!" Kate called, catching a glimpse of Hannah's astonished face as she pelted off, running flat out towards the sound of the screaming. She let her feet take her pounding down a smaller footpath, then onto an unlit lane. Adrenaline spiking, she ran just as she had when she was training with Olbeck for the half marathon two years ago, steadily but quickly, trying to see through the gloom. Up ahead she could just about make out two figures, one staggering about, one crouched by the side of the road. The screams came from the crouching figure. The staggering shape was uttering sounds that were almost worse; guttural, choked cries and moans.

"Are you hurt?" gasped Kate, skidding to a stop by the crouching shape – a teenage girl; she could now see even in the darkness. The girl had both her hands clasped in her hair and her mouth was an open, vibrating hole. "Can you hear me? Are you hurt?"

The girl didn't answer but her screams faded into whimpering gasps. Kate turned to the other person, who was still staggering from one side of the lane to the other, weaving like a drunk, holding his hands out in front of his body in a peculiarly stiff-armed way.

As Kate got nearer, she became aware of the smell. She stiffened, nostrils flaring. The teenage boy with his arms held away from his body stopped and looked at her, panting. She could see the whites of his eyes through the darkness of the street.

"What's wrong? Can you tell me what's wrong?"

The boy's voice was hoarse. He almost whispered. "In there. It's in there. I – I didn't realise... I fell..." He started to cry.

Kate turned at the sound of running footsteps behind her; Jay and Laura arrived at the scene, panting.

"What's going on, sis?" Jay asked between puffs. Laura said nothing but immediately headed towards the crying girl and crouched beside her, putting an arm around her shoulders and talking to her comfortingly. God, that girl is good in a crisis, that's for sure. Kate had a fleeting thought that she might try to recruit her.

"I don't know yet. You wait with him," she said, indicating that Jay should stay with the boy.

He nodded and approached him, flinching a little when he got close enough to smell him, but managing to keep his voice calm and even. "You all right, mate? Don't worry, don't worry, you'll be fine..." Even as he spoke, he was reaching for his mobile and dialling. What a difference a few years made, thought Kate. Back when Jay was in his teens, he wouldn't have called the police if he'd been kidnapped by Jeffrey Dahmer. Now Kate could hear him steadily relaying what little information they had to the dispatcher on the other end of the phone line. Good lad; Kate was proud of him. She reached for her keys and the little pen-sized torch she kept on the key ring.

The smell got steadily worse, invading her nostrils as she approached the open door of the derelict cottage. What on Earth were these kids doing down here? Kate tried not to breathe as she nudged the door open with her elbow, shining the little beam of the torch in front of her. Even though she was expecting it, the state of the body was still a shock. What was left of what had once been a person – it was impossible to tell whether it had been a man or woman – lay in the middle of the floor, surrounded by a lake of dark fluid. Had the poor kid actually fallen into the body? The poor bastard. Kate had to take a quick breath to fill her bursting lungs and almost retched. She retreated back out of the front door, leaving it slightly ajar, not wanting to touch anything with her bare hands.

WITHIN HALF AN HOUR THE lane was transformed; strobed by blue flashing lights on the attending police vehicles and the ambulance that had been ordered for the traumatised teenagers. Kate had sent her little group home, not without some grumbling from Jay that he was missing all the action. She stood waiting for Anderton, reaching for her phone every so often to call Olbeck before remembering with a curse that he was sunning himself on a beach in Barbados, the jammy git.

Scene of Crime officers arrived. Kate nodded to Stephen Smithfield, who headed the team and she'd worked with several times before. She was more pleased than she thought she ought to be at the sight of Anderton's car drawing up and pulling in to park at the side of the lane.

"Evening, sir," she said, as he made his way over to her. He was dressed more casually than she was used to seeing him, in a rather nice shirt and jeans, and had the air of a man pulled reluctantly from an enjoyable social engagement. Had he been at the Great Wyrm festival? Surely not. "Sorry to interrupt your evening."

Anderton rolled his eyes. "Par for the course, Kate. Par for the course. What have we got?"

Kate told him as they walked towards the cottage.

When she got to the part about the male teenager, Anderton whistled. "He fell *in* it? The poor little bugger. He'll not get over that in a hurry."

SOCO had set up powerful lights that illuminated the scene with a brilliant white glow. The body looked diminished, even more pathetic than it had been in the dark. Anderton, observing from the doorway, didn't say anything but his eyebrows rose. "The paths will have their work cut out for them," was his only remark.

Kate hadn't thought of that, and it was then she realised that her ex-boyfriend, Andrew Stanton, would probably be doing the post mortem. Her heart sank. Would she be able to get Olbeck to go instead of her? Then she remembered, again, that he wouldn't be back from Barbados for another couple of days, the jammy *git*.

"It may not even be a suspicious death," Kate remarked, as she and Anderton watched the SOCOs do their work. Camera flashes momentarily dyed the air in the room an even brighter white. "Could have been a homeless guy who just died naturally."

"Yes, that's true," agreed Anderton. "We won't know anything more tonight."

Just as he said that, there was a sudden flurry of interest in the room. One of the technicians held up something in an evidence bag. Kate squinted. "What have you got?" she called.

"Syringe," the woman holding the bag called back. "Several syringes, actually."

Kate and Anderton looked at one another. "There you go," said Anderton. "Common or garden overdose. Not for us."

"You can't know that for sure," protested Kate.

Anderton blew out his cheeks in a sigh. "No, I know that. But I was dragged up here from a very nice dinner engagement that I would really rather like to get back to. Stick around for another hour or so if you want, Kate, but I don't think there's anything for us here."

Dinner engagement? With who? Kate was aware of a rather unpleasant prickling sensation, a swoop of her stomach, as if she'd stepped into a plummeting life. Dinner engagement with *who*? Not that it was any of her business, but...

Anderton said his goodbyes and left the cottage. Kate muttered a goodbye in response and turned her eyes back to the scene, barely comprehending it. She and Anderton had had a one night stand, several years ago, and she couldn't avoid her powerful attraction to her boss. Nothing else had happened between them since, but Kate wondered – far too often for comfort – whether Anderton's feelings for her were in the dim and distant past or, like hers for him, merely under the surface, waiting for the perfect chance to erupt again.

She sighed and made an effort to focus on what

was happening in the here and now. After another half an hour, Stephen Smithfield came over, pulling off his gloves. "Hi, Kate, you still here?"

"Someone's got to be."

"What happened to Anderton?"

Kate shrugged. "He had to get back somewhere. Can you give me any more info on the body?"

Stephen nodded. "This is all very preliminary, you understand. You'll have to wait for the PM for the details. But based on the clothing and the size and shape of the body, I would estimate that it's a man, probably middle-aged. He's been dead for several weeks. In fact, judging by the insect activity, we could be talking months."

"He's been here for months? Undiscovered?" Kate raised her eyebrows. "You're sure about that?"

"Call it two months," said Stephen. "But don't quote me."

"Cause of death?"

"Again, this is just ballpark. There's no obvious signs of violence. No blunt instrument lying nearby, no ligatures, no knives. And you know we found those syringes. I think you're looking at a natural death."

"Well," said Kate, "far be it from me to do myself out of a job, but let's hope so."

"If it turns out to be a heroin overdose, which is looking likely, we might be able to narrow down the time of death. Amazingly, you know, certain drugs can actually significantly affect the rate of larval development. Fascinating, really."

"Is that right?" asked Kate, hiding a grimace. "Well, I'll guess we'll see what the PM throws up. Thanks, Stephen. I'm going to head off now."

"Enjoy the rest of your evening," said Stephen, without evident irony. Kate grinned to herself as she walked away. Techs were a little weird, you couldn't get away from that. Nature of the job, she supposed. She pulled her jacket a little more firmly around herself – a chilly wind had suddenly sprung up – and made her way back to the main road.

Chapter Two

"MORNING, TEAM," ANDERTON SAID, CLEARLY in ebullient mood as he crashed into the office. "Hope there aren't too many sore heads from the festivities last night. Kate, I know *you'll* be all right. What's the latest on our very, very dead body?"

Kate snapped her mouth shut in the middle of a yawn. Yes, she wasn't hung over – she didn't really drink – but she'd still only managed about four hours of sleep. Needless to say, Jay, Laura, Hannah and Dan had pounced on her the second she'd walked through the door of her house, wanting to know every gory detail. She'd not been able to tell them much but they had still insisted on staying up late into the night, hashing over the events of the evening and wondering who the poor man or woman had once been. Kate, conscious that the smell from the corpse had permeated her hair and clothes, had finally pleaded for mercy and jumped in the shower, only to find that Jay had drained the hot water tank in his own frantic ablutions. Eventually, she boiled the kettle and had a very unsatisfying strip wash in the bathroom before everyone eventually succumbed to weariness and she could finally get to bed.

She hauled herself into a straighter sitting position. "There's no ID as yet – it seems likely that they'll have to go off dental records, or even DNA, which means we'll have to wait for the PM."

"And that is taking place...?"

Kate fought back another yawn. "Tomorrow."

"Fine. Hopefully we'll have an answer then and we'll also know whether we're even taking on the case. If it's an accidental death, nothing suspicious, then that's not our department. God knows we've got enough to do without worrying about careless junkies."

There were a few smothered grins at that but Kate was conscious of a twinge of annoyance. They didn't yet know for certain whether this was a suspicious death, did they? For the first time, she wondered whether Anderton's mind was completely on the job. He seemed, well, a trifle hasty to dismiss this case.

She realised Anderton was still speaking to her. "Kate, would you mind doing the PM tomorrow, seeing as you're already involved with the case?"

Kate was all set to protest. She knew very well that it would probably be her ex-boyfriend, Andrew Stanton, conducting the post mortem and that would be rather awkward. On the other hand, nobody else seemed at all interested in taking this on. She should be responsible for it, if only to make sure that nothing was missed.

"Yes, I'll do it," she confirmed, with a small inner-sigh. It might not be be Andrew conducting the examination, after all.

Anderton nodded, apparently satisfied. "Anyone else got anything?"

Theo raised his hand. "We've done some preliminary interviews with the neighbours, not that there are really any neighbours to the cottages. There's a few houses fairly nearby though, on the other side of the river, and we've had a couple of reports that the cottages were used by vagrants, homeless men. One in particular was spotted there several times a couple of months ago. Nothing hugely conclusive though, no names or anything."

"Okay, fine. Thanks, Theo. Anyone else?" Silence fell across the room. Anderton shrugged. "Okay, well, let's break it up. If anyone needs me, I'll be in my office for the next hour."

Everyone drifted back to their desks. Kate spent a moment conferring with Theo and getting a description of the man the 'neighbours' had mentioned. Armed with that information, she spent an hour scrolling through the records of the various homeless people who'd made it onto the database for one reason or another, before she stopped, annoyed with herself at not immediately realising that without knowing the age or the sex of the body they'd found there was no point in printing off any records for comparison. She'd just have to wait for the post mortem tomorrow before doing anything else. She swung her chair back from the desk a little, frustrated and a bit bored.

By this time it was lunchtime and she made her way to the canteen. Normally she ate with Olbeck, or occasionally with Theo and Jane, but today she didn't feel much like being sociable. Having a house full of visitors meant that she was feeling the need for a bit of solitary peace and quiet. She bought a salad and a carton of orange juice and took it away from the hubbub of the canteen, deciding to eat it in the little park just over the road from the police station.

She passed through the main entrance and reception of the station on her way out and paused for a second by the main desk, checking she'd put her pass in her hand bag. There was a man standing by the front desk on the visitor's side; a non-descript man, short and rather slender, and with the kind of thin moustache that hadn't been fashionable since the 1940s. Kate only noticed him because of his air of nervousness and the way he was shifting from foot to foot.

"What was that again, sir?" asked Sergeant

Brown, who was currently manning the reception desk.

"I *said*, I wish to report a robbery," the little man replied. His voice was high with nerves, or perhaps naturally that way.

"Can you give me a few more details?" asked Sergeant Brown.

The little man hesitated for a second. "*Here*? Give you the details here and now?"

"Well, just so I can see how best we can help you—" began the sergeant, but the man made a sound that was almost a squeak and then began backing towards the door, shaking his head.

"I changed my mind – it doesn't matter – I don't... I changed my mind—" he stuttered and then turned and fled.

In the silence that followed, Kate and Sergeant Brown exchanged meaningful glances. Then, rolling his eyes to the ceiling, the good sergeant sat back down again and Kate smiled and made her way outside. On the steps, she caught sight of the little man, almost running, turning a corner down a side street before he scurried out of sight.

Kate had forgotten all about the incident by the time she returned from her lunch break. She checked her emails, noting with pleasure that she had one from her friend Stuart, once a colleague and now a private investigator, suggesting lunch next week. She replied to him in the affirmative and made a note in her diary. It would be good to have someone to run this latest case by, seeing as Olbeck wasn't around.

The phone on Theo's desk rang. Concentrating on her emails, Kate just about registered that he'd answered it. After a moment, the tone of his voice pierced her consciousness and she raised her head, looking across the desk to where he held the phone wedged between his ear and his shoulder, nodding and making notes.

KATE HESITATED, LISTENING. SHE COULDN'T have put her finger on what exactly was being conveyed from the other end of the phone, but her copper's sense was tingling. Something had happened.

She waited until Theo had put the phone down and raised her eyebrows questioningly at him across the desk.

Theo winced and stretched his neck. "What?"

"What was that? And you shouldn't take a call with the phone like that, you'll bugger your neck."

"You're telling me," Theo said with feeling. "Anyway, it's nothing much. Couple of bodies found but – wait a minute—" he cautioned as Kate tried to interject. "Doesn't look suspicious at all. Common or garden overdose."

Something about the phrase made Kate sit up a little. Who had said that? She remembered then –

it had been Anderton, at the scene last night. And here it was again. More overdoses?

"So who was that?" she asked.

"Uniform. They're just reporting."

"*Two* bodies found?"

"Yeah, I know. That's the only thing that's a bit strange. Why are you so interested, anyway? Do you want to go and see?"

"Yes, actually, I do," Kate said slowly. "Are you coming?"

Theo shook his head. "Nope, you can have this one. It's probably nothing, anyway."

"Well, maybe," said Kate. She picked up her bag and said goodbye, rummaging for her car keys as she left the office.

Her al fresco lunch had done her good; she felt more awake. Kate lowered the car window to get the full benefit of the lovely weather. She hoped the Indian summer would continue for a good few weeks yet. She thought, with a touch of slightly malicious enjoyment, that it would be rather good if it held *right* up until Olbeck and Jeff touched down at Heathrow tonight and then broke into torrential rain. Then she'd have the pleasure of telling them what they'd missed whilst they were swanning around Barbados.

Chuckling to herself, Kate swung the car into a side street in the suburb of Arbuthon Green. She could clearly see which house she should be heading to – there was a uniformed officer standing outside, fending off enquiries from curious passers-by. Blue and white crime scene tape had been stretched over the front of the driveway. Kate parked the car and locked it. She showed her badge to the officer on guard and ducked under the tape. She didn't recognise him but that wasn't unusual; Abbeyford had recruited a lot of new personnel in the last year. The house itself was a charmless sixties box made of pale yellow brick with a red-tiled roof. The small front garden was badly overgrown, the white trumpet-shaped flowers of bindweed twining their way through the uncut privet hedge. The front door, covered in peeling pale blue paint, stood open. Kate poked her head tentatively around the frame. Through the cluttered hallway, she could see more officers standing in the living room, observing something that was currently out of her sight.

"Hello?" Kate walked further in. She recognised one of the uniformed officers, Sergeant Bill Osbourne, and shook his outstretched hand. "Hi, Bill. What have you got?"

Osbourne indicated with a nod of his head. "Two bodies. Not sure it'll be for you, though, Kate. Looks pretty unsuspicious to me."

Kate followed his gaze. The bodies of two young men sat opposite one another, in a rather eerie mirroring of each other's posture. Both were sat upright but slumped, each with a tourniquet around their left arm and a syringe deeply embedded within the crook of their elbow. Both had their eyes closed, both were pale as milk, the skin of their faces already beginning to blotch with decay.

"Well," said Kate. She bit her lip, pondering. "I have to say you're probably right. Overdose."

"Aye," said Osbourne. "Pretty straightforward."

"It's a bit odd that they both died at the same time," said Kate. "Isn't it?"

Osbourne shrugged. "Not if the drug was unusually pure. If they shot up together at the same time, it would have been quick. Neither of them would have been aware of the other, I would have thought."

"I suppose you're right," said Kate. "I guess there's nothing else..." She looked about, hoping for inspiration. "A gas leak?"

Osbourne chuckled. "You're clutching at straws, lass. The PM will confirm what we suspect, but I'd be stunned if it was anything other than a straightforward overdose."

Kate sighed. "Yes, I'm sure you're right." She looked again at the bodies, feeling a queasy pity. "Who are they?"

Osbourne consulted his notebook. "Pete Hardew and Wayne Potter. Known addicts, petty criminals, no great loss to society."

"Right." There didn't seem to be much more to say. "Well, I guess there's not much point me hanging around then, is there? Could you let me know if anything surprising does turn up?"

"Aye, will do, Kate."

"Thanks, Bill." Kate said goodbye and turned to leave the fetid little room.

Chapter Three

OLBECK WAS BACK IN THE office the next day, ridiculously tanned and relaxed looking. He handed around bottles of rum and hot pepper sauce – Kate took the sauce – and suffered half-teasing, half resentful remarks about 'glad you decided to finally come back', 'beach got too boring for you, did it?' and all the usual clichés. After everyone had finally settled down and got back to work, Olbeck came over and perched on Kate's desk, swinging one leg.

"So, what have I missed?"

"Not a lot, actually," Kate admitted. She turned her chair to face him. "God, you're so brown. We've had several dead bodies but nothing too untoward, apparently."

"*Several* bodies? Tell me more." Olbeck listened as Kate outlined the last few cases. "It's a bit weird that they've all started popping up now, isn't it? Or could it just be coincidence?"

"You tell me," said Kate. "The thing is, Anderton's not interested, which means that it's not top priority. He's kind of just chucked it at me to keep an eye on."

"Right." Olbeck rubbed his tanned chin and got to his feet. "Well, keep an eye on it then, and let me know if anything untoward actually turns up."

"Aye-aye, captain." Kate threw him an ironic salute. "So when am I going to see the photos, then?"

"When I put them on Facebook, of course."

"I don't do Facebook."

"I know you don't, you Luddite. Tell you what, I'll have a grand cinema screening over at our place sometime soon and you can see them then."

"Marvellous."

Olbeck cautiously scratched at his nose, which was peeling. "What are you up to today?"

Kate grimaced. "I've got the PM on the body from the cottage."

"What fun for you."

"Indeed." Kate got up herself and began to gather her things together. "And guess what's even *more* fun? Andrew's doing the PM."

Olbeck winced. "Ouch. Awkward."

Kate hoisted her bag onto her shoulder. "Don't suppose you want to do it for me?" she asked, cheekily.

Olbeck gave a cynical laugh. "Nice try, but no."

"Oh well." Kate gave him another salute. "I'll go and face the music then. See you later."

Driving towards the pathology labs, Kate's

expression of false cheer collapsed and she groaned. Seeing Andrew was just *so* awkward. Doctor Stanton was still obviously very hurt by Kate ending the relationship on such spurious – at least from his perspective – grounds and, whilst he was too much of a gentleman to go so far as to make pointed and cutting remarks, there was a stiffness to his manner, a marked contrast to the easy flirtatiousness that used to characterise their interactions. Kate fervently hoped that the scheduling of the post mortem had been changed, or – even better – that Doctor Telling had replaced Andrew as the one performing the procedure, but it was not to be. Kate checked in at reception and made her way to the theatre, swearing under her breath.

As it happened, Theo was already there. Kate was left relieved that there was another person there to temper the frosty atmosphere but also annoyed that he'd beaten her to it. Theo had been promoted to Detective Sergeant last year, and whilst he and Kate worked better together now than they had at first, their partnership had nothing of the easy familiarity that Kate used to enjoy with Olbeck. Kate took a deep breath, greeted Andrew with as nice a smile as she could, and vowed that she would spend the evening hard at work studying. She was due to take the exams for her Inspector's certificate in three weeks' time, and – *please, God* – if she passed them then she and Olbeck might be back working together again.

Once the PM was actually underway, some of the tension in the room eased a little. Andrew had always had a rather terse, abrupt way of working, which meant that any undercurrent of resentment went virtually unnoticed. Kate could concentrate on the job at hand, watching as the sad remains of what had once been a human being were probed and weighed and measured and the mystery of their death hopefully cleared up.

"Your victim is male," Andrew said, bending over the table. "I would say late forties, perhaps older. Early fifties maybe."

Kate nodded. "Any chance of fingerprints?"

Andrew risked a glance at her. "Not a hope. I think your best bet will be dental records, although we'll be able to do DNA tests as well. There might be a match."

Kate nodded again and fell silent whilst Theo asked a few more questions. She normally found post mortems hard, particularly if the victim had been young, but this one was turning out to be less emotionally draining than normal. The body was so badly decayed it was almost unrecognisable as a human being, and detachment came surprisingly easily.

Eventually Andrew stood up, easing his shoulders back with a groan. Kate was uncomfortably reminded that she used to give him back massages when he came home from work. She swore, yet again, never to get involved with anyone else she might be likely to have to work with in future. It never ended well. Inevitably, her thoughts flew to Anderton. Something was different about him lately. He seemed...younger, somehow. More *invigorated*. Kate frowned, and concentrated on what Andrew was saying.

"...not possible to ascertain a definite cause of death," he continued. "There's a plethora of further tests to be run though and I'm hopeful that one of those will have the answer. You can read up about it in my report."

"Thank you," Kate said hurriedly. He gave her a stony-faced glance and merely nodded before leaving the room. Kate sighed.

"Dear, oh dear," Theo said with a tinge of malice. "You're not very popular here at the moment, are you, Kate?"

"Oh, sod off," Kate said, picking up her bag. "How's *your* love life these days, anyway, Theo?"

Theo looked smug. "Doing nicely, thank you. Why, want to join the harem?"

Kate laughed, despite herself. "It's tempting but...no."

"You don't know what you're missing," Theo said as they left the building together.

"Oh, sod off," said Kate again, but this time she was grinning as she said it.

"Well?" Olbeck asked after Kate returned to the office. "Get a name?"

Kate shook her head. "Nope. We'll have to wait for dental records. We don't even have an official cause of death yet."

"Drugs overdose," Anderton said over her shoulder, making her jump. She hadn't heard him come up behind her which, given Anderton's usual mode of conduct, was something of a miracle. "I keep telling you. Mark, have you got five minutes?"

Olbeck got up. Kate watched them both walk out and slowly went back to her desk. She felt uncomfortable; frustrated, a bit bored, unsure of what to do next. Unenthusiastically, she began to deal with the paperwork that had accumulated over the past couple of days. She checked her emails, noting that she had one from Bill Osbourne, which made her perk up a little until she realised he was just letting her know about the post mortems for the two bodies found in Arbuthon Green. Well, she wouldn't be going to those. One session with Andrew's unspoken resentment was enough for her, thank you very much.

She became aware of the growling of her stomach and realised that it was nearly two o'clock and she'd not yet eaten any lunch. She considered the canteen but it was a lovely day and perhaps a quick sandwich in the nearby park would restore her enthusiasm. Kate picked up her bag and made her way out of the building, passing through the main station reception area as usual. There was a man standing at the front desk, but the only reason Kate noticed him was the phrase he used, identical to the one used by that funny little man who'd changed his mind about reporting a crime.

"I want to report a robbery."

The moment Kate heard that, she recalled the earlier occasion. She stopped and listened.

"A robbery, sir?" asked the desk sergeant.

The man nodded. He was tall and broad-shouldered, with curling black hair and a rather rakish goatee. Kate, moving closer, thought he would make an excellent pirate.

"Yeah," he was saying. "Definitely a robbery. I'd rather not give you all the details right here, though. That a problem?"

"That's fine," said Kate, stepping smartly up to the counter. Both the man and the sergeant looked a little startled. "I can take this, Sergeant. If you'd like to come with me, sir?"

The man grinned, showing a lot of healthy white teeth. His gaze swept from Kate's face to her chest, down to her feet and up again. "Hell yeah, officer. Lead on."

Kate knew she should be offended but instead

she felt like laughing. He was just so obvious it was almost a refreshing change from the usual sly ogle. She led him to a vacant interview room and shut the door, gesturing for him to sit down.

"Now," she said, taking the chair opposite him. "I'm Detective Sergeant Kate Redman. What can I do for you?"

The man's grin grew wider. Wolfish, Kate thought to herself. The big bad wolf. It made what he had to tell her even more strange.

"I need to report a robbery," he said, quite easily, as if he were commenting on the weather. "It feels kind of strange to be telling a woman this, though. Not that I'm complaining," he added hastily. "I never thought I'd be one for the whole 'doing my duty' thing, but it kind of feels like that's what I'm doing, you know what I mean?"

Kate was lost. "Sorry, sir, you'll have to start from the beginning. You were robbed?"

The man nodded. "Yeah. I'm Jack, by the way, Jack Harker. Yeah, I was robbed. It's kind of a strange story though."

Kate smiled brightly. "Well, why don't you try me?"

Jack Harker looked around, as if there were someone else in the room, and then leaned forward conspiratorially. "I was at this bar, in town, last night. Twenty One. You know it?" Kate nodded as if she did, and he went on. "So, I'm having a few drinks, having fun, you know what I mean? These two chicks rock up. Sexy girls, young – you know?" Kate raised her eyebrows and he said hastily, "Not *too* young, early twenties, or something. Foreign. Think they were Eastern European or something. Had that really sexy accent. Anyway, we get talking and drinking and we end up back at my place."

KATE NODDED ENCOURAGINGLY, ALTHOUGH SHE wondered where this story was going.

Jack Harker continued. "Anyway, we're getting down to it and I pick up my drink – that's about the last thing I *do* remember – and the next thing I know, it's dark and I'm cold and I'm all alone in my living room, tied to a chair."

There was a moment's silence. Kate re-settled herself into her chair and cleared her throat. "You were tied to a chair?"

She would have sworn that Jack Harker was one of those rare human beings incapable of blushing, but a faint rosy hue became visible beneath the dark stubble of his cheeks.

"Yeah," he said awkwardly. "Seriously, they drugged me and left me tied up in a chair. I was fucking freezing, surprised I didn't die of exposure."

"Okay," said Kate, after a moment. "You believe you were drugged – something in the drink, presumably? – and then robbed. What did they take?"

"My wallet, credit cards. A bit of cash I had in the house. My iPad, my laptop. Everything, really."

Kate let her eyes fall to the notebook she was ostensibly making notes on. "Would you recognise these women again, if we managed to make an arrest?"

Jack Harker frowned. "I don't know. They were dark. Long haired, small, sort of thin. A bit thin for me, actually, but, you know..."

"What were their names?"

Jack Harker grinned a little sheepishly. "I can't remember."

Kate folded her lips, trying to hide her own smile. "It's probably not important, sir. They almost certainly gave you false names anyway, if they were planning to rob you."

"Right. Yeah."

"Have you seen your doctor? Or been to hospital?"

"No. No, I'm fine. Just a bit of a headache."

Kate leant forward a little. "I really would encourage you to get checked out. Just in case."

"Okay." His eyes flickered upwards for a moment and she knew he had no intention of doing what she suggested. Oh well, his loss.

She whisked through the rest of the formalities, gave him a crime identification number, and handed Jack Harker back to the desk sergeant. He tipped her a wink as he was led away to another interview room and she was unable to stop herself smiling back in response. Then she chastised herself as she turned away. Keep your mind on the job, Kate. The rumbling of her stomach made her realise she really did need some lunch now. She collected her handbag and made her way out of the building, dismissing the handsome Mr. Harker from her mind.

Chapter Four

KATE ARRIVED AT THE OFFICE earlier than usual the next day. Bathed in a glow of righteousness, she was somewhat annoyed to find that Olbeck had beaten her in by some time, judging by the multiple empty coffee cups lined up by his keyboard. She flung her bag under her desk and switched on her computer. While waiting for it to warm up, she wandered over to Olbeck's office and leant against the door frame. "Want a coffee?"

"Already had three." Olbeck was hunched over his keyboard, typing furiously. Kate watched him for a moment. There was something different about him, but infuriatingly, she couldn't quite put her finger on what it was. New haircut? She dismissed the idea. New suit? No, not that either. What was it?

Olbeck came to the end of whatever sentence he was typing and looked up. "What's up?"

"Nothing," Kate said, straightening up from her slouch. "Just wondering what you're doing?"

Olbeck looked surprised. "Nothing exciting. Why?"

"No reason..." Kate said nothing more as Olbeck's phone rang.

He picked it up with his customary greeting. "DI Olbeck here."

Kate watched. From the nature of Olbeck's comments, she gathered it was something serious. She saw his eyebrows raise at one point. She should be starting work but she didn't move. She had the feeling something important had just happened.

Eventually, Olbeck put down the receiver. Kate looked at him expectantly.

"Okay, okay," said Olbeck. "You know what that was, don't you?"

"Suspicious death," Kate said; a statement rather than a question.

"Got it in one." Olbeck hesitated a moment and then added "It's Trixie Arlen."

Kate's eyes bulged. "Seriously?" she managed, after a moment.

"So patrol says." Olbeck and Kate looked at each other for a moment in mutual shock. "That's what they said. They're at her house now."

Kate found her voice. "Wow. Seriously, Trixie Arlen?" She was silent for a second and then asked "What happened?"

Olbeck was gathering up his coat and keys. "Nothing tangible, as yet. They just called in to say

Trixie Arlen's been found dead at her home, that's all." He looked up. "Will you come with me?"

"Er – *yes*," said Kate. "Of course I will."

ON THE DRIVE THERE, KATE tinkered with her phone, trying to bring up the Wikipedia page that covered Trixie Arlen's career, both the early glory years in her days as a Nineties 'It' girl and the most recent times with her reinvention as fertile earth mother, *Good Housekeeping* columnist, and luxury kitchen products designer. The signal out in the deep countryside where Trixie Arlen's farmhouse was situated was terrible and Kate, kept tutting and swearing as the page failed to load and then reload.

"Don't worry about that now," said Olbeck eventually. "There's probably nothing there that's particularly accurate anyway."

Kate conceded and put the phone away. "I remember her being on that chat show," she said. "Do you remember? *Wicked Weekend*?"

Olbeck winced. "God, the nineties..."

"I was about fourteen," said Kate, grinning. "How old were you when that was on?" she asked, mock-innocently.

Olbeck looked pained. "I was precisely four years older than you," he cleared his throat and went on, with dignity, "as you well know. And yes," he continued, looking a little more sober. "I do remember that. And when she lost her first husband and lost the baby..."

Kate's smile fell from her face. "Oh," she murmured. "I'd forgotten about that."

"Well, she bounced back," said Olbeck with an ironic grin. "Didn't she? I remember all the papers from that time. All about the phoenix rising from the ashes and all that bollocks."

"I'd totally forgotten about the baby," Kate said, and although she said it quietly, there was something in her voice that made Olbeck look over at her momentarily.

They drove on in silence for a few minutes. They followed a route into the deepest Somerset countryside, the roads gradually narrowing from A roads to B roads, and then to a road that was barely a farm track, hemmed in both sides by the sun-bleached cow parsley, brown bracken and the spreading tentacles of brambles, heavy with berries ripened in the September sun. Up ahead, Kate could see police tape cordoning off the entrance to another lane, crumbling brick columns standing sentinel on either side of the tarmac.

Olbeck showed his ID to the uniformed officer guarding the entrance to the gateway and they were waved through. Olbeck proceeded cautiously, mindful of the time he and Kate had almost been obliterated by a speeding ambulance on the way to a crime scene. They proceeded on this journey without mishap, passing an orchard, a pond and a field of waving wheat, before drawing up in front of a comfortable, shabby sort of house that nevertheless managed to convey an air of wealth, despite its peeling paint and Bohemian aspect. The farmhouse itself had been much extended, and a large silver Range Rover was parked at one side of the circular driveway. There was a building which had clearly once been a stable block, now converted into a garage, which held another black Range Rover and a new model Mini. Thick ropes of wisteria hung over the front of the house, framing the front doorway in drooping fronds of green.

Olbeck and Kate made their way inside, nodding to the constable who guarded the front door. The hallway was tiled in slate, the walls painted a soft green, an antique console table by the front door. A wire basket held children's shoes and wellingtons, and a canvas shopping bag, printed with a fashionable mid-century design, was hung from the peg rack up on the wall.

Kate and Olbeck followed the murmur of voices and the click and whirr of the crime scene cameras through the house. They glanced into the kitchen, where Kate saw more uniformed officers; a man in an expensive suit sat at the kitchen table with his head in his hands, a blonde woman, red-eyed and sniffling, sat beside him. That was all she could take in in a swift glance before they continued on through a comfortable and understatedly luxurious sitting room and then a playroom crammed with every conceivable toy, finally ascending a flight of stairs to the first floor.

The bedroom they found themselves in was large and square, dominated by a huge bed with a black iron frame. A grey silk counterpane had slipped to the floor and the bed itself was unmade. Trixie Arlen's body lay on top, half on her side, one arm dangling from the bed, almost brushing the soft pile of the carpet. Kate and Olbeck paused in the doorway, silently regarding the scene. Doctor Telling had already arrived and was leaning over the body, her deft, gentle fingers already measuring, probing, testing. Kate sent up a silent prayer of thanks that Andrew hadn't been the pathologist on call and then chastised herself for being so unfeeling.

Several Scene of Crime officers were already working the room and Kate and Olbeck stepped forward a pace or two and then remained still, to allow them to work undisturbed. Doctor Telling noticed them and nodded a silent greeting before turning back to the body.

"It *is* her, isn't it?" Olbeck asked in a murmur.

Kate nodded uncertainly. She could see it was Trixie Arlen; that face was instantly recognisable from a thousand different television and press appearances, but she could understand Olbeck's hesitation. Trixie looked...diminished, somehow;

shrunken, reduced. But that was understandable. Death was the great leveller, and Trixie's beauty had always depended heavily on her natural vivacity. She had been cute rather than sexy; rather gamine, the girl-next-door type – *a nice girl, attractively wholesome, good clean fun* – in the media's stereotypical clichés.

Kate looked at Trixie's dead face. More so than usual, the scene felt unreal; a stage set of a crime scene rather than a real one. Was it because the victim was so famous? Kate recalled her first reaction to Olbeck's news – violent disbelief. Celebrities led charmed lives, didn't they? Things like this didn't happen to them – not to the ones who didn't walk on the wild side.

Kate let her gaze rest on the body, trying to take in as much information as possible. Trixie was dressed in grey marl leggings and a loose pink T-shirt. Her hair – that famous mop of bouncy brown curls – tumbled around her face, partially hiding it. Kate could see the wink of something sparkly in an earlobe, but she wore no other jewellery that Kate could see, except the huge diamond solitaire engagement ring and the plainer wedding band on the hand that dangled from the bed. The tips of her fingers on that hand were already purple with lividity.

There were no obvious signs of violence; no stab wounds, no ligature marks, nothing to indicate a violent death. Was this even a suspicious death? Kate tried to think back on what little she knew of Trixie Arlen from the papers. Had she had any health problems that she'd shared with the media? Kate thought she could recall something about Trixie having fertility treatment; how in God's name had she managed to retain that bit of trivia? She didn't even *read* gossip magazines. That was everything she could recall. Momentarily, she remembered the lost baby that Trixie had suffered after the death of her first husband, musician Ivo Wright. A miscarriage at eight months – wasn't that technically a stillbirth? Kate winced inwardly. Poor woman, what a trauma that must have been.

She came back to reality with a start, realising that Olbeck and Doctor Telling were already conferring. Kate hurried over to join them by the bedside.

"Can you give us any indication at all?" Olbeck asked.

Doctor Telling peeled the surgical gloves from her long, thin fingers. She placed them neatly inside the pocket of her overalls and turned to pick up her medical bag.

"I'm not quite yet ready to give a definitive answer," she replied quietly. Doctor Telling always spoke quietly; Kate wondered, irrelevantly, if she and Mr. Telling ever had a really good, flaming stand-up row. Doctor Telling continued. "There are several indications as to a probable cause of death but I really don't want to commit myself before there's been a proper post-mortem. I'm sorry," she added, as Olbeck opened his mouth in protest, "but in a case that is bound to be as high profile as this one, I really can't be seen to get anything wrong."

"Fine," Olbeck said, clearly annoyed but able to understand her point. "Can you tell me whether you think it's a suspicious death or not, at least?"

Doctor Telling paused in the doorway. She shook her head. "I'm almost certain that it isn't, but that's all I can say at this point. I'll be doing the post mortem tomorrow and I hope to see you and DS Redman there. We can discuss it all thoroughly then."

They had to be content with that. Once Doctor Telling had left to arrange procedures for transporting the corpse to the pathology labs, Kate and Olbeck turned back to look at the body. It still had that same sense of surrealism about it. Kate fought the urge to reach out and touch it, just to check it was real. She stepped back a little and let her gaze swing around the room. Again, it was comfortable, well furnished, all in expensive but conventional good taste. A large wardrobe at the side of the room held seemingly enough clothes to fill a department store. There were several framed photographs on the dressing table, a family shot of Trixie, her husband and three young, cherubic-looking children. Several other individual shots of the children, twin boys and a younger sister from the looks of it.

Kate's fingers itched to start searching, burrowing through drawers and belongings and under the huge bed, but of course she couldn't. Olbeck was gesturing that they needed to leave the room to the SOCOs and Kate concurred. They made their way back down to the kitchen.

"Who found the body?" Kate asked as they walked down the stairs.

Olbeck ducked his head to avoid a low beam. "Her husband. He was away last night, on business apparently. He got home very early this morning and found her. The children were still asleep, thank God."

Kate stopped walking. "The children were *here*? All along?"

Olbeck nodded, his face grim. "I know. Imagine if they'd gone into her room and found her..."

"God," Kate closed her eyes momentarily. "Thank God her husband came home in time. Is that him in the kitchen?"

"Yes. Shh, we're almost there." Olbeck opened the door to the kitchen, which had been closed since they passed it earlier.

The black-suited man had raised his head by this time and was staring across the kitchen table, his face a blank, stony mask. The blonde woman beside him had stopped crying. She sat quietly, occasionally giving an exhausted gasp, as if she'd suddenly run out of air.

"Mr. Jacob Arlen?" asked Olbeck, quietly. The suited man stood to face them. Olbeck held out his hand and Arlen shook it automatically. "I'm Detective Inspector Olbeck and this is my colleague, Detective Sergeant Redman. I'd just like to convey our sincere condolences for your loss. Do you feel able to answer a few questions? It can wait, if you don't feel up to it."

Arlen hesitated. Then he shook his head and said in a low voice, "No. No, it's fine. It may as well be now."

"Thank you. Do you mind if we sit down?" At Arlen's nod of assent, Kate and Olbeck seated themselves at the scrubbed pine table, Kate facing Arlen, Olbeck facing the blonde woman. Arlen introduced her as 'Kyla Mellors, a good friend of ours.'

"Are your children still here, Mr. Arlen?" Kate asked. She devoutly hoped they'd already been removed to a safe and familiar place.

"My parents came and got them," Arlen said, and Kate inwardly sighed with relief. "I don't know how much they – I mean, I don't know how much they know. I was in such a state of shock I think I... I think I just said that Mummy was ill and they could see her later—" His voice broke. He put his fist to his mouth, as if his clenched fingers could stop the tears that Kate could sense were just below the surface of his ostensible control. Kyla Mellors reached out a tentative hand and Arlen, after a moment, took his fist down from his face and clutched at her fingers. "I'm sorry," he said after a few moments. "I know that doesn't help. I'll try not to – to break down again."

Olbeck murmured the usual soothing platitudes and Kate added hers. Kyla Mellors was visibly wincing at the strength of Arlen's grip on her hand, and after a moment he seemed to realise it, releasing her with a 'sorry – sorry, Kyla'. She nodded and smiled wanly but Kate saw her slip her hand beneath the table and thought she was probably rubbing away the pain with her other hand.

"If you could just take us through what happened, Mr. Arlen," Olbeck said. "I understand you were away on business last night?"

Arlen nodded. "Yes, that's right. I often have client meetings after normal office hours and last night I knew I'd be so late home that it wasn't worth me travelling back. I booked a hotel and left very early the next morning. This morning, I mean."

"Your office is in London?"

Arlen nodded again. "Yes, in the city. On Cheapside."

"Were you due to go back to work today?" asked

Kate. "It seems an awful lot of travelling to be home for a few hours."

Arlen frowned. "I just wanted to see my children for a few hours, I see them so infrequently during the week that I take the opportunity when I can. My first meeting today wasn't until eleven am, so I knew I'd be able to be home for an hour or so, to help with the children's breakfasts and getting them ready for nursery." A thought seemed to strike him. "My God, I haven't told the office yet, I didn't think... I'd better call my assistant."

"That's fine, Mr. Arlen," said Olbeck. "I suggest you do that sooner rather than later. But I would strongly suggest you don't go into too much detail as to why you're unable to get to work. Unfortunately there's going to be considerable press interest and it would be good to head them off for as long as we possibly can."

Arlen looked shaken, as if that reality had only just occurred to him. "Yes. Yes I can see that."

Olbeck gave him a moment and then gently prompted him again. "You arrived here very early this morning."

"Yes, about six o'clock. The traffic can be appalling later on and I wanted to miss it if possible. Thank God I did come back so early...if the children had woken..." Arlen trailed off and there was a moment's silence.

"And what happened when you arrived home?" Olbeck asked patiently.

Arlen closed his eyes momentarily. "I unlocked the front door and let myself in. I was as quiet as possible – I didn't want to disturb anyone. I can't remember exactly what I did first – oh, yes, I put on some coffee. Then I went upstairs to change, and I walked into the bedroom and found – found Trixie. I...I gasped, I think, or made some sort of sound. I could see she was dead straight away. I – I was so shocked. I didn't really know what to do—"

"Did you touch the body, Mr. Arlen?" asked Kate.

Arlen winced. "Yes. Yes, of course I did. I had to check whether she was – whether I'd made a mistake." His head dropped forward and his voice lowered. "I knew I hadn't, though. She was so cold – I knew I was too late."

"What happened then?" asked Olbeck.

"I think I – yes, I called the police then, or an ambulance. I dialled nine nine nine. After I put the phone down I...I panicked a bit – I remembered the children and I thought for one awful second—" Arlen shut his eyes again and shuddered. "I thought for one awful second they were *all* dead, they'd all been killed or somehow died together." He shuddered again, leaning forward and Kyla took his hand once more. "I ran to their rooms and they were okay, thank God, thank God. Manon woke up then, and I took her downstairs and put her in her high chair." Kate blinked a little at the daughter's name. *Manon?* Arlen continued. "I locked our bedroom door so the boys wouldn't go in when they woke up. Then I – I just waited for the police to get here. They were the ones who suggested I call a friend."

"So he called me," said Kyla, speaking for the first time. She had a low, attractive voice. Kate wondered whose friend she had been; Trixie's? Arlen's? Or a true mutual friend? Kate studied her a little more attentively. Kyla looked to be about thirty-five, although she could have possibly been older. She had long, highlighted blonde hair, well-shaped dark eyebrows and good cheekbones – the striking looks of an ex-model. She too wore a wedding ring and a large multi-jewelled engagement ring.

Olbeck jotted down a few notes and looked up. "May I ask how long you've been married, Mr. Arlen?"

"Five years. We met a few years after Trixie's first husband died."

"Did your wife suffer from any health problems, any medical issues that you were aware of?"

Arlen frowned but after a moment, he answered. "No, nothing that I'm aware of."

"When was the last time you spoke to her?"

"I called her yesterday, at about five o'clock, to tell her I wasn't coming home. There'd been some uncertainty as to whether I'd be able to make it home that night or not, and I wanted to let her know that I wouldn't be able to make it."

"How did she sound?"

Arlen's eyes closed again briefly. "She sounded fine. Absolutely normal. I asked her if she had any plans – sometimes she went to the gym or to yoga in the evenings if she had a babysitter – but she just said she was going to have a quiet night and probably go to bed early."

"So everything seemed absolutely as normal?"

"Yes."

Kate had thought of something. "Mr. Arlen, your wife is a very famous person. Is she active on social media at all – Facebook, Twitter, that sort of thing?"

Arlen nodded. "She loved Twitter, she was on it all the time. She always used to laugh and read me the tweets that amused her."

"Thank you. If you could give me the details of all of her social media accounts, that would be very helpful," Kate said and Arlen nodded.

Olbeck turned to Kyla Mellors. "Mrs. Mellors, you might be able to help us as well. Did you speak to Mrs. Arlen at all yesterday?"

Kyla shook her head. "No, not yesterday. We met up for coffee the day before. Just a quick catch up, you know."

"Did you often do that?"

Kyla withdrew her hand from Arlen's once more. Kate watched her fingers twist together. "Quite often," Kyla said, with a break in her voice. "About once a week or so. I've got a daughter the same age as Manon – that's how we met, at an ante-natal class – and we often used to get the girls together for play dates." Her voice shook quite badly now, tears trembling on the edge of her eyelids. "I can't believe this has happened, it doesn't seem possible." She fell silent with a gasp and put her trembling fingers up to her mouth.

Feeling cruel but pushing on anyway, Kate asked her a question. "So, you were close friends? Would she confide in you?"

Kyla Mellors struggled for a moment. "I suppose so," she said eventually, with another gasp. After another moment, she appeared to regain some control. "We used to talk about all sorts of things. She'd had an interesting life."

"Indeed," said Kate. "Could you have said whether there was anything worrying her? Did she seem concerned or anxious about anything?"

Kyla appeared to give the question serious thought. "I don't *think* so," she said eventually. Her hand went up to her mouth again and she bit her thumbnail.

Kate's eyes narrowed. Something about Kyla's last statement didn't ring true. She sat up a little, wondering whether to push the questioning, but Olbeck was already talking. Kate sat back. She decided that asking more probing questions now would probably be counterproductive. There would be time enough for that later. And besides – maybe this would all be cleared up after the post mortem. Briefly, her thoughts went to Bill Osbourne; she must get in touch with him and find out what the findings of the post mortem on the two young men were.

For a moment, Kate experienced that sudden sense of surrealism again. She couldn't really be sat in *Trixie Arlen's* kitchen, could she? She, Kate Redman, couldn't really be questioning Trixie's bereaved husband? Her gaze slowly tracked the room as she listened to Olbeck asking Arlen for details of his firm and the hotel he'd stayed in last night. It was a large kitchen, the units obviously made to measure by an expensive firm, the floor slate-tiled, every accoutrement well made, costly and suitable. But for all that it was a homely place, full of family clutter and a refreshing lack of pretension. Kate recalled the first case she'd ever worked in Abbeyford, the kidnapping of the Fullman baby and the murder of his nanny. She remembered that house – that hideous, vulgar, new-money house – with no expense spared but no taste either. This house was very different. There was mess; toys everywhere, paperwork scattered over the kitchen countertops. Kate could see crumbs on the floor, muddy footprints by the back door that were too small to have been made by an adult, an overflowing kitchen bin in the corner. Her eyes went to Jacob Arlen. It was funny; he didn't look like the kind of man who would relish living in domestic chaos. He was clean-shaven and good-looking in a stern, ascetic way, trim for a man who had to be well into his fifties. Was this his first marriage? What must it be like for a middle-aged man to have a relatively large young family? He was a hedge-fund manager, or something like that, Kate recalled – something deadly dull but extremely lucrative. Had Trixie Arlen out-earned him or was he the breadwinner?

Olbeck wrapped up the questioning. He and Kate handed over their cards and took their leave. They walked back through the hallway and out into the space in front of the house. The sun blazed overhead, bright enough to make both of them screw up their eyes. Kate was amazed afresh at how nature just went on doing what it did, no matter what small, petty human dramas were being played out on the stage it provided The sun would travel slowly across the sky and set in the west, and night would fall and then the sun would rise again, and it would be the day after Trixie Arlen died. The day three children lost their mother would be over and gone, never to come again. She blinked several times and reminded herself to get a grip.

"Come on," Olbeck said. "Let's have a look around."

Kate followed him as he crunched over the

gravel, round the side of the farmhouse. A flash of reflected light caught her eye and she looked over the gently rolling fields to the lane where cars were gathering. Figures with cameras were emerging and clustering at the gates. The paparazzi were here. Corpse flies, Kate thought with a scowl as she followed Olbeck around the corner of the house.

Chapter Five

KATE HAD SEEN MANY TERRIBLE things at various post-mortems. She'd seen bodies with ragged, gaping knife wounds; bodies with skulls crushed like empty egg shells; bodies burned so badly that they were barely recognisable as the remains of a human being. She'd been sickened and disgusted and angry in turn. But until Doctor Telling looked up from the body of Trixie Arlen and told Kate how she believed the woman had died, Kate realised she'd never been truly shocked. Not until now.

"A *heroin* overdose?" Kate was so flabbergasted for a moment that she couldn't think of what else to say. "You're...you're *kidding* me."

Doctor Telling, who rarely smiled, flashed her a slightly ironic one. "That surprises you?"

Kate put her hands up to her head and dropped them. "It surprises me? It bloody *stuns* me. Trixie Arlen, a heroin user?"

Doctor Telling stood upright, easing her back from the tension of several hours of stooping over the body. She slowly peeled the rubber gloves from her hands and dropped them into a yellow hazardous waste bin over by the sink. She nodded. "I had an inkling that that was how she died when I first saw her at the scene," she commented. "I noticed the puncture mark on her inner elbow straight away. Of course, I didn't want to say anything then and there. It could have been that she was on some other form of injectable medication or that she'd had a recent inoculation."

"I am absolutely *stunned*," Kate repeated. She looked at Trixie Arlen's blank face on the gurney. Doctor Telling was skilled at making a corpse appear as lifelike as possible; it was somewhat uncanny, but Trixie Arlen looked less dead here on the post mortem table than she had done lying on her own bed. For all that though, she didn't look as if she were sleeping. Whatever it was that had made her human had gone, and this outer shell was all that was left.

"You're absolutely certain it was heroin?" asked Kate, still without taking her eyes off of the body.

"No. No, not at all. I can't say that with any certainty – you'll have to wait for the results of the toxicology tests. But there were old injection marks on the body, between her toes and within the groin area."

Kate grimaced. "It just seems so incredible. She's

– she *was* a mother of three. I know she was a bit wild in the nineties but...it just seems incredible."

There was a knock on the glass panel of the theatre door and they both looked up. Olbeck was waving at them, in a 'can I come in?' type of gesture. Doctor Telling raised her own hand in acknowledgement and he pushed open the door.

"Morning, ladies. Sorry I'm late."

Doctor Telling nodded. "Good morning, DI Olbeck. I've just been telling DS Redman the findings of the PM."

"And?" Olbeck adjusted the sleeve of his jacket. "Anything concrete?"

Kate was dying to be the one to tell him but it would be the height of bad manners to override Doctor Telling in her own workplace. She clamped her lips shut, watching Olbeck's face as Doctor Telling delivered the news, and saw the expression on his face mirror that of her own as she'd been informed.

"Bloody hell," said Olbeck, which was as close as he ever came to swearing. "I must say I'm surprised."

"You and me both," said Kate, unable to keep quiet any longer. "The press will have a field day."

Olbeck frowned. "Which is precisely why we're going to inform them that the results were inconclusive. Right, doctor?" Doctor Telling inclined her head in acquiescence. "There's no point stoking any more wild rumours until we get the results of the tox tests back, right?"

"Right," said Kate. They all looked at Trixie Arlen in silence.

"Oh," Doctor Telling said suddenly and the two officers looked at her quickly. "There's one more thing that struck me. She had some quite serious bruising on her upper right arm, almost as if she'd been gripped very hard. I thought that might be significant."

Olbeck's eyebrows rose. "Indeed. You think it was inflicted by someone else?"

"Yes. It's quite distinct. Have a look for yourselves." The two officers watched as the doctor lifted the sheet covering the body and indicated the bruising. Kate could see for herself the pattern of purple-blue blotches on Trixie Arlen's slender arm.

"I see," said Olbeck. "Well, that's something to take into consideration."

It wasn't until they had said goodbye to the doctor and were walking down the corridor towards the exit that the implications of what Doctor Telling had told them suddenly hit Kate, as if from a great height. She actually gasped under the impact and stopped dead.

"What is it?" asked Olbeck, turning back to her.

Kate looked at him, wide-eyed. "If Trixie Arlen

died of a heroin overdose, then why didn't we find any drugs paraphernalia on or near her body?"

Olbeck's face looked as though he'd just walked into something. "Bloody hell." His face flickered again and Kate knew he was just realising that he should have seen that straight away. She couldn't help a small inner stab of triumph that she'd clocked it before he had. "You're absolutely right, Kate. I should have seen that."

Kate began walking again, a little faster than before. Olbeck hurried to keep up. Kate spoke to him over her shoulder. "We're not mistaken, are we? There was nothing there, nothing at all. Just the body."

"No, nothing. Well, if there had been it would have been obvious, wouldn't it? We would have known how she died straight away."

"I know, I was just wondering if we'd forgotten it." Kate remembered the two bodies at the house at Arbuthon Green, mirror images of one another, sat there with the syringes still in their arms. She felt, just for a moment, a tremor of something too insubstantial to put a name to – some tiny flicker of comprehension that slipped away almost before she noticed it. She came to a halt at the car, shaking her head in frustration.

"You all right?" Olbeck asked as he drew out his own car keys.

"I'm fine," Kate said impatiently. "We've got to get back and let Anderton know."

"I'll let him know," Olbeck said, and although his tone was neutral, Kate thought she heard something of a warning in it, a reminder that Olbeck was, in fact, her superior officer. She was conscious of a spurt of shame and then something very much like anger. It wasn't like him to pull rank. She pressed her lips together and got into her car.

"WELL, WELL, WELL," SAID ANDERTON, pacing the floor as was his habit. "We finally have a crime scene, ladies and gentlemen. Typical that it has to be the most high profile celebrity that we've ever had to deal with. The press will be trying to get everything they can on this one, so I'm sure I don't need to remind you that you speak to nobody without my say-so, and you don't discuss anything – anything at all – with your nearest and dearest."

"Trust nobody," said Olbeck, with a grin.

Anderton looked at him without smiling. "That's right, Mark. And if I find anyone leaking anything to anyone, they'll be out the door so fast their arse won't touch the ground. Do I make myself clear?"

Everyone nodded, grim-faced. Kate, momentarily distracted, thought that Anderton was looking particularly handsome today. His thick grey hair had obviously recently been trimmed and he was wearing a well-cut new suit. She blinked, bringing herself back to listen to what he was saying.

"Now I'll recap quickly for those of you who weren't at the scene. Trixie Arlen, former TV presenter and 'It' girl of the nineties – most of you younglings will only know her from her cookbooks and kitchen products range – was found dead at her home yesterday. No sign of forced entry, no sign of violence, no sign of foul play. The doctor at the scene thought it was a non-suspicious death and the PM seemed to confirm that. We're still waiting for results from the labs for the toxicology tests, but it seems likely that Trixie died of a heroin overdose. That's not yet been made public." Anderton reached the wall and pivoted on his heel. "Now, the problem with that is that we found nothing with the body that indicated that she'd been injecting. No syringes, no actual drugs, no paraphernalia, nothing. Can anyone tell me what that might mean?"

Kate raised her hand. She'd spent most of the night going over one scenario after another and Anderton could have them all if he wanted. "She might have been shooting up with somebody else. When she overdosed, they panicked, cleared everything away and fled."

Anderton nodded. "That's a very likely possibility. Anyone else?"

Kate opened her mouth to go on but Theo got there first, as he often did. Kate gritted her teeth.

"She could have been alone when she died but someone found her and took the stuff away. Her husband, probably," said Theo.

Anderton had paused in his pacing and was scribbling frantically on a whiteboard. "Right, another good possibility. So we've got X, the unknown who might have been with Trixie when she died. We've got Y, the unknown who found the body and cleared away the stuff. Anything else?"

Kate raised her hand hurriedly before Theo could speak. "Someone could have been with her and left her *before* she overdosed."

Anderton was still scribbling. "So, this Z might be innocent of clearing any drugs, etc. away but could have still been with Trixie that night?"

Kate nodded. "Say that's how it happened and then, in the morning, her husband comes home, finds her dead and for whatever reason clears away the evidence of what killed her."

"Right," said Anderton. "Could be, could be. Anything else?"

There was a moment's silence. Then Kate said slowly, "Trixie could have been with someone who left before she died, as I said before. That person or someone else could have come back later, or even earlier in the morning than her husband, and cleared everything away. So her husband might not be implicated."

"Phew," said Anderton. "The plot most

definitely thickens. Right, well, all of this gives us a firm starting point." He began to tick points off on his fingers. "We need a thorough search of the farmhouse. We need forensics on who's been in that bedroom and whether anyone can be eliminated. We need to know how quickly after injecting Trixie died and whether she could have moved to her bedroom from somewhere else in the house. Sod it, we need forensics from all over the house. And we need to start digging at alibis. I want Jacob Arlen re-interviewed as a matter of urgency."

People were standing up, preparing to move. The room began to hum with that slight sense of urgency and bustle that the beginning of a case could induce. Kate adjusted her shirt sleeve, which was slightly twisted, and recalled that something else that needed to be mentioned.

"Sir?" She had interrupted Anderton mid-flow and he frowned.

"What is it, Kate?"

Kate reiterated what Doctor Telling had said about the bruising on Trixie's arm. "She said it looked quite distinctly as if someone had grabbed her there."

Anderton was still frowning. "Which arm?"

For a moment, Kate groped to remember. "The right one," she said, thankfully.

"And she injected into her left arm?"

74

"I think so. I'd have to re-read the report to be certain."

Anderton had stopped writing. He let his gaze sweep over the room. "Could you find out, Kate? Quickly?"

"Yes, of course," said Kate, slightly confused by the seriousness of his tone.

"Because," he went on, as if reading her mind. "If someone had hold of her by the arm which she was using to inject herself, could it be that she was actually forced to do it?"

The buzz of activity in the room stilled. Kate felt a small chill at the thought. If someone had forced Trixie Arlen to inject herself with a lethal dose of heroin then that would make her death...murder.

She could see by the expressions on the others' faces that the same thing had just occurred to them. Anderton cleared his throat. "Now, I'm not saying that that's what *did* happen. It's another possibility, that's all. But we mustn't discount it."

He began allocating various tasks to various people. Kate half listened, distracted by an image in her head; a large hand on Trixie's arm, strong fingers clamping a full syringe into her hand, forcing the needle into her skin, making her depress the plunger. Then nothing; oblivion. Could it have happened like that? Did that make more sense than thinking that a respectable, middle-aged, *famous* woman would actually voluntarily inject herself with a lethal street drug while her young children slept in the next room?

Kate came to with a start, realising that the room had emptied of everyone but Theo. He was busy pulling on his coat and fiddling with his phone.

"Am I with you?" asked Kate, walking over.

"Ha, ha," said Theo. "You almost had me there."

"No, seriously," said Kate with a shamefaced grin. "I was away with the fairies for a moment. What am I supposed to be doing?"

Theo rolled his eyes. "Of course you're with me, you dozy mare. We're doing the farmhouse search. Come on."

"Oh, right," said Kate. She tried to hide her disappointment. She knew Anderton and Olbeck would probably be doing the interview with Jacob Arlen and she would have much rather sat in on that. She thought she had a talent for interviews, for sniffing out when a suspect was lying or, at the very least, concealing something. Searching was all very well but... She let her train of thought trail away as she followed Theo out to his car. A secondary thought occurred to her - that she really *must* get some studying done. Her exams were coming up in less than a fortnight. Pass those, and she wouldn't be relegated to digging through farmhouse bedrooms, that was for sure.

THE CROWD OF PAPARAZZI AT the gate of the Arlen

farmhouse was so dense that Theo had to slow to a crawl and eventually sound his horn several times to make any kind of progress. The two uniformed officers who were guarding the gate opened it for them to pass through and, looking back as they drove through, Kate saw them physically repel a particularly bold photographer trying to sneak it after them. She didn't envy them their job – she could just imagine the kind of remarks they were being subjected to as they stood there guarding the gate.

The house was empty. Arlen and his children were clearly staying elsewhere and Kate didn't blame them. It had only been three days since Trixie Arlen died but already a kind of grimness was settling on the house, along with a fine film of dust. The colours of the furniture and the pictures and ornaments seemed dulled, the gleam of glass and metal muted, and as Kate and Theo walked towards the stairs, their footfalls seemed more muffled than the carpets warranted.

They began in the bedroom. Kate took the bedside table first, a little delicate white-painted thing. On the top of it lay the latest issue of Vogue, a magazine that Kate had never seen the point of. Fashion bored her rigid, although she was clearly in a minority. Shaking it out, she laid it on the bedclothes, which still bore the imprint of Trixie Arlen's body. Kate felt a moment of nausea that was unusual. She turned back to the bedside cabinet, opening the drawers and unearthing a set of high-end sex toys that made her raise her eyebrows.

"Blimey. Theo, look at this." She held up a vibrator that could almost have been a work of art, a modern sculpture, perhaps.

Theo laughed. "Well, you never know, do you? I always thought that sort of shit stopped when you got married."

"Well, what would *you* know about that?" said Kate, suddenly annoyed at his tone. She laid the toys on the bed next to the magazine. She suppressed the little voice inside her that told her *she* didn't know anything about being married, either.

The cabinet didn't yield anything else of interest. Kate knee-shuffled over to the chest of drawers that stood against the far-side wall. That too was clearly expensive, a lovely mahogany antique. Kate began to work methodically from the top down. She could hear Theo open the wardrobe door behind her and the clank of hangers as he began to sort through the clothes inside.

The drawers held a lot of underwear, most of it surprisingly functional, given the discovery in the bedside table; Kate had expected to find scraps of black lace and little silk nothings, but most of what emerged was sturdy white cotton. The brassieres were mostly the type that enabled breastfeeding. She pulled each drawer fully out, searching right to the corners. She made sure to check underneath each one – sometimes people taped things to the bottom, a surprisingly effective hiding place for something thin enough to be concealed there – but her efforts yielded no results. Kate worked her way through the rest of the drawers, finding nothing more exciting than cashmere jumpers, multiple pairs of black and grey leggings and skinny jeans.

She and Theo rolled back the rug beside the bed, looking for trap doors or secret hiding places beneath the floor boards. Kate moved backwards slowly, on her hands and knees, scanning the boards for barely visible openings. She found none. They stripped the bed of its coverings and checked the mattress, and then the springs of the bedframe. It was a bed made of black wrought iron, sham-vintage, made to look old.

"There's nothing here," said Theo, eventually. "Let's move to the en-suite."

Kate had been tapping her fingers against the black bars of the footboard. "Wait," she said, suddenly aware of the hollow sound emanating from beneath her hands. "Wait a minute."

She looked carefully at the top of the footboard, which was actually a long rail which ended in the two posts which held up the foot of the bed. Each post was topped in a kind of curling iron flourish. Biting her lip, Kate tested one of them, twisting it gently left. It resisted for a moment and then yielded, unscrewing smoothly. Once it had come off in her hand, Kate held her breath and looked down into the hollow space that was revealed.

It was right there, near the top of the bed leg, stuck to the inside of the tube with sellotape. She reached it with her gloved fingers and drew out a small plastic bag, half full of brownish powder. She and Theo looked at each other.

"Well, well," said Theo. "So she was a junkie after all."

Something about his tone flicked Kate on the raw. "You don't know that," she said crossly. "We don't even know what's in it yet."

"Oh, come on."

Kate held the plastic packet pinched between two gloved fingers. She dropped it into an evidence bag and sealed it. That brief moment of anger flickered and died. She felt sad. "Well, you're probably right," she said quietly. "Let's check the other one."

Theo did that while Kate fetched a torch to look further down the exposed pipe of the bed leg. She didn't find anything else there. Theo also found nothing in the other leg. They renewed their search of the room with more enthusiasm but found nothing else suspicious.

They scoured the en-suite bathroom next, Kate starting with the mirror-fronted bathroom cabinet on the wall over the sink. She found several bottles of prescribed anti-depressants with Trixie's name on the pharmacist's label. There was an enormous quantity of luxury skincare and make up – literally boxes of it – in the only other cupboard in the room. Perhaps Trixie had been given some of it for free? Kate couldn't imagine how anyone would manage to get through this amount of makeup in a lifetime. She caught sight of the own face in the mirror and rubbed at her cheeks, frowning. She looked pale and tired. There were a pile of glossy fashion magazines in a rack by the toilet and topmost was one that made Kate stare and then extend a hand to pick it up. Trixie Arlen – yes, she hadn't been mistaken – was the cover star. Kate looked at her picture; the bouncing glossy curls, the glowing skin, the flash of white teeth. A memory of Trixie's body on the pathology table popped into Kate's head and there was something obscene in the juxtaposition. How could someone who looked this vital, this healthy, actually be a heroin addict? Was it possible?

Searching the children's bedrooms was somehow worst of all. Kate tried not to wince as her gloved fingers lifted out piles of neatly folded clothing, leaving them in brightly coloured heaps on the striped rug in the middle of the floor. The twin boys shared a room, two cot beds facing one another with matching duvet cover sets. Blue and white bunting hung on the wall and a little nightlight, shaped like a boat, stood on a small table between the cots. Kate didn't like to think of a mother, a parent, hiding drugs in their pre-schoolers' room, but you couldn't deny that it sometimes happened. She found nothing though and, relieved, went through to the little girl's nursery to search. What was her name again? Something weird. *Manon*, that was it. Kate paused in the doorway blinking, taking in the excess of pink. It was as if a giant ball of Disney princesses had exploded. She took a deep breath and began the search, again finding nothing.

After several more weary hours she and Theo called it a day, the single bag of powder the only thing that resulted from a whole day's search. They locked up the house, setting the alarm. They crawled their way back through the crowd of paparazzi; still as many, if not more, as had been there that morning. When would they get fed up of waiting? Kate thought of the headlines still to come, of the moral outrage that would result once the reality of Trixie's death was known. She winced inwardly and put her head back against the headrest of the car seat. Theo put his finger out to turn the stereo on and then seemed to change his mind, sighing a little. They drove back to the station in tired silence.

Chapter Six

THE NEXT MORNING, KATE REGARDED her desk with something akin to dismay. The surface had all but disappeared beneath a teetering pile of cardboard folders, slippery plastic envelopes, dirty coffee mugs and veritable strata of loose paper. She thought of everything she had to do and fought the urge to push her chair back and flee the room for good. Instead, she squared her shoulders, attempted to push the toppling piles of paperwork into some sort of order, and gave thanks that she'd actually treated herself to a 'good coffee' for once.

Theo, who sat opposite her, kept interrupting his own work to seize his mobile phone and swipe at the screen. Kate, whose own concentration was interrupted every time he did it, gritted her teeth until she couldn't hold back a barbed comment any longer. "Waiting for the football results, are you?"

Apparently, the bitchiness went straight over Theo's head. "No," he said absently. "I'm just checking the headlines. I want to see what they're reporting on Trixie Arlen's death."

Kate felt a little ashamed of herself. "Oh," she said. She got up and went round to his desk, leaning over to look at the little screen herself. "Anything interesting?"

"Nah. The usual sentimental guff, family's heartbreak, bringing up her tragic life, you know the kind of thing."

"Her tragic life?"

"Yeah – you remember, her first husband died, didn't he, and she had that miscarriage."

"Oh, yes," said Kate. "What *did* he actually die of?"

"Drugs overdose."

Kate's eyes widened. "Seriously?" She was silent for a moment, thinking. "That actually might strengthen the case that Trixie was a drug addict herself. I mean, suppose her first husband introduced her to drugs?"

Theo nodded. "But suppose it was the other way round? If you'd lost a loved one to heroin, why the hell would you start taking it yourself?"

Kate got up and went back to her own chair. "That's a good point," she admitted, sitting back down. "I don't know enough about addiction, really – the psychology of it, I mean." Briefly, she recalled her mother's struggle with the bottle. Perhaps she knew more than she realised. "I'll look into it," she said, half to Theo, half to herself.

The phone rang when she was halfway through a Google search for drug and alcohol treatment centres in Abbeyford. Impatiently she snatched it up. "DS Redman here."

"Oh, hello." She recognised the quiet tones of Doctor Telling. "I have some information on your John Doe. We've received the reports back from the dental lab."

Kate's head was so full of Trixie Arlen that for a moment, she had to struggle to recall who on Earth Doctor Telling was talking about. Then she remembered – the first body they'd found, in the abandoned cottage.

"Oh, yes, thanks," she said. "Do we have a name?"

"Yes, the dental records brought up a match. His name really was John, John Henry Miller, born in 1960 in Aberdeen. Should I send over the files?"

"Oh, please do," said Kate. She felt a little glow of satisfaction in the news. She hated the cases – and there were always a few – when a body went unidentified, unclaimed, unmissed. What an awful way to end up, with literally no one on Earth to mourn you. "Thank you very much, Kirsten."

"It's no problem," the pathologist replied in her quiet tone, but Kate thought she could detect an answering measure of satisfaction in her voice. Doctor Telling was gentle and empathic, like all the best doctors. Kate felt a moment's regret that; because of her break up with Andrew, she'd lost the chance of getting to know Doctor Telling better. She'd always felt that she would be a nice woman to be friends with.

"Is there anything else back from the labs with regard to the Arlen case?" she remembered to ask, but the answer was negative. Kate hadn't really expected a result yet – these things always took more time than anticipated.

The morning's work took on a more upbeat feel after the call. Kate flew through a load of outstanding paperwork, arranged an appointment with one of the directors of Outreach, Abbeyford's largest drug and alcohol treatment centre, caught up with her emails, and realised with a start at twelve o'clock that she was supposed to be having lunch with Stuart. She had to grab her coat and handbag and make a run for the café where they were supposed to be meeting, arriving five minutes late and looking more dishevelled than she would have liked.

Stuart was already there, at a table by the window. He caught sight of Kate as she hurried through the door and gave her a grin. She puffed up to the table, panting apologies.

"It's not like you to be late," Stuart said, leaning over to kiss her cheek.

Kate dropped into a chair, trying to smooth her hair. "I know. I've been flat out. Sorry."

"I remember." Stuart had worked as an undercover officer for the Abbeyford team before a catastrophic series of events had led to his resignation, and he now worked as a private detective. Although he put a brave face on it, Kate knew that he missed working for the police, but she'd learned by now not to mention the possibility of Stuart reapplying for the force.

It was funny, she thought as she took a menu from the hovering waitress, how differently she felt about Stuart now than when she'd first met him. She'd almost hated him on first sight, thinking him arrogant, pushy and rude. Of course, he could still be all of those things, she thought with an inner smile, but somehow it didn't seem to bother her anymore. He was clever and funny and good company. Olbeck kept muttering about how she and Stuart would make the perfect couple and why wasn't she doing anything about it, but Kate knew he was wrong. She appreciated Stuart's friendship and that was all; she hoped he felt the same way about her.

They gave their orders and then settled back in their chairs.

"So," said Stuart. "What's new?"

Kate told him what she could about the latest cases, the three heroin overdoses and the Trixie

Arlen case. She mentioned that she'd made an appointment to talk to a drugs counsellor, to try and get a bit more insight into what made an addict do the things that they did.

"I can't help feeling that I should understand a bit *more*," she said, stirring her leek and potato soup. "I keep thinking that there might be a connection to these overdose cases. Well, of course there must be. How could there not be?"

Stuart swallowed a mouthful of food. "Yeah," he said. "You're on the right track. First thing you should do is pull some stats, don't you think? Get the analysts to do some digging. Find out the rate of overdose deaths last year – last month, even – and do some comparisons with the most recent cases."

Kate brightened. "That's a great idea. Thanks. I'll do just that."

"No charge," said Stuart, grinning. "You've got a name for the first body, right?"

Kate nodded. "Yes, we have. That's something I'll be looking into when I get back." She finished the last mouthful of soup, pushed her bowl away a little, and relaxed back into her chair. She looked across at Stuart. "It's funny, but I can't help thinking about Trixie Arlen." She opened her mouth to mention the one suspicious packet that she and Theo had found, and then recalled Anderson's warning. Of course, Stuart didn't know, and he *couldn't* know either, not from her. "It's so sad, isn't it?" Kate said hastily, covering herself. "It's always more sad when there are children, don't you think?"

"I suppose so," said Stuart. He appeared to be thinking about something. He reached out to spin his water glass in a slow circle. "It wouldn't surprise me..." he began and then stopped.

"What?" asked Kate.

"Well," said Stuart. "It wouldn't surprise me if the Trixie Arlen case is connected to these heroin deaths. It wouldn't surprise me at all."

"Really?" said Kate, as casually as she could. "What makes you say that?"

"Oh, you know. Sudden death of a healthy, relatively young woman. A woman known to have associated with heroin addicts in the past – her first husband, for one. She was pretty wild back in the nineties, wasn't she? All those rumours." Kate was uncomfortably aware that he was keenly watching her face. He was too good at reading people, damn him; it was his undercover training. "I don't suppose the PM threw anything like that up?"

"No," said Kate, truthfully. "It was inconclusive."

"So you're waiting for toxicology results, right?"

"That's right."

Stuart sat back in his chair and stretched. "I bet you a tenner I'm right. No, wait. If I'm right, next time we have lunch, you're buying."

Kate smiled reluctantly. "You know I don't

gamble, Stuart. But I don't mind shouting you lunch."

Stuart laughed and, thankfully, Kate could see him dismissing the subject. "Can't believe you don't gamble. Don't you have Irish heritage? It should be in your blood."

"That's why," said Kate, standing up to leave. "Thanks, anyway. Let's meet up soon, yes?"

"You got it."

They hugged goodbye and Kate made her way back to the office, thinking about what Stuart had said. He was right. Why had she been so shocked by Doctor Telling's findings on the pathology table? Her, a seasoned police officer? With a pang, she recalled that Stuart had lost a brother to heroin addiction, years ago. No wonder he was more attuned to the possibility. She wished she'd remembered that at the lunch so she could have talked to him about it. But perhaps that would have been too painful.

Kate ran over the details of the case in her head. Even if Trixie had been an addict, it wasn't that straightforward, was it? What about the bruising on Trixie's arm? Kate pondered the questions as she walked back to her desk. Who had cleared away the syringes, the drugs, the tourniquets? She wondered whether Anderton had interviewed Jacob Arlen yet and whether anything interesting had come to light. She had a flashback to sitting at the Arlens' kitchen table, watching Arlen's face as he recounted his journey up to the bedroom, through the silent house, to find his wife's dead body on the bed. Kate remembered the blonde neighbour, the friend – what was her name? Kyla Mellors – and the slight hesitation in the woman's answers. There was something there, something to be further investigated. It could be nothing, but then again... Kate added *interview Kyla Mellors* to her ever-growing checklist of things to do.

DOCTOR TELLING HAD EMAILED THROUGH the information on John Henry Miller and Kate spent the rest of the afternoon reading through it. He'd been born in 1960, had gone to school in London, and joined the army at sixteen. Reading between the bare facts, Kate could see a man who'd lost his place in the world once he left the Armed Forces – a sad fact that was more common than people thought. There were several reports which detailed his arrests for vagrancy, for being drunk and disorderly, for possession of a class A substance. She flipped forward to the photo that Missing Persons had forwarded. A non-descript man, weathered by years of rough living, brown eyes, greying hair. Someone had obviously reported him missing at some point, for MISPER to have his details, but who? And did it really matter? Kate did a quick calculation and worked out that his parents were almost certainly dead, given his age. Was it worth trying to find out? This wasn't even their case anymore.

After a moment, she slowly clicked the mouse to close the PDF and exited the email, with a faint feeling of guilt. She wondered how long Miller had lain dead in that cottage. Had he actually died from the overdose or had he succumbed to exposure, lying there comatose in the filth and the cold? It was horrible to think of, almost as horrible to think that there was no one left to mourn him. She made a resolution that she would go to his funeral. She would probably be the only one there, apart from the celebrant, but that made it even more important. Kate made a quick mental note to find out when the council-funded funeral would be.

Miller's grizzled old face kept recurring to Kate that night as she relaxed at home. She had lit a fire, the first of the season, as the warm autumnal weather had suddenly given way to a chill. Her living room was neat, as usual, and filled with objects of comfort and sentimental value. She should have been happy, or at least relaxed, but somehow the image of the derelict cottage kept intruding, Miller's remains in a nauseating puddle on the filthy floor. *Unwept, unhonoured and unsung...* Kate poked up the fire, lit an expensive scented candle that she'd kept 'for best', and wrapped herself in a woolly throw. The crackle of the burning logs sounded too loud in the silent house and she felt the weight of the empty rooms above her. She tried putting on some music but it seemed to just make things worse – an echo in the void. Oh, get a grip of yourself, woman, she told herself, but in the background, all she could hear was the same word, repeated over and over again. *Alone.*

She passed a bad night and got up the next morning feeling as though she hadn't slept. Olbeck, by contrast, almost bounced into the office, tousling Kate's hair as he passed her desk, which made her swat him away in annoyance.

"What's up with you?" she asked grumpily, sliding out of her chair and following him to his office.

"Nothing," said Olbeck, grinning. "Just full of the joys of spring."

"It's October."

Olbeck dismissed her comment with an airy wave of his hand. "Full of the joys of autumn, then. Hey, you doing anything next week? Thought you might like to come for dinner."

Kate felt a pang of anxiety, despite her tiredness. "I've got to study, actually. My exam's coming up soon."

"When?"

"On the fourteenth." Kate felt a stronger pulse of nervousness. She'd hardly done any studying at all. What had she been thinking? She straightened up a little and vowed that studying and only studying was what she would spend every spare waking moment doing.

Olbeck rummaged in his desk. "Right, right," he said. Kate wondered whether he was even listening. "No problem."

"Let's make it a date after my exams," Kate said, feeling that at least that would be something to look forward to afterwards.

"Hmm?" Olbeck looked up and blinked. "Oh right, yeah. Let's do that."

Kate rolled her eyes and went back to her desk.

"You look knackered," Theo observed, busy at his computer.

"Gee, thanks," said Kate. She rubbed her face and tried to get her work head on. "Did Anderton interview Jacob Arlen yesterday?"

"Nope, don't think so."

"Anything else I should know about?"

"Don't know. Haven't even seen the boss yet."

Kate sighed. "Anything from forensics?"

Theo reached for a pile of folders. "Now, that I can help you with. Here you go."

Kate opened the first file and did her best to follow it but the scientific jargon blurred in front of her tired eyes. She made herself and Theo another coffee and tried again, making notes of her own. She murmured the names under her breath.

"Fingerprints found in the master bedroom of the farmhouse were those of Trixie and Jacob Arlen, their children, Kyla Mellors, another child's and an unknown female." Kate read through the list again. The unknown child could well turn out to be Kyla Mellors' daughter, although that would have to be checked. But the unknown female...?

She really needed to talk to Anderton but, as before, he seemed to be absent from the office again. Had he ever been so hard to get hold of? His office was empty and his mobile went straight to voicemail. Kate emailed him and left a post-it note on his computer, hoping to cover all bases. She grabbed a salad from the canteen and ate it back at her desk, still wading through all the forensic reports from the Arlen case.

That night, Kate attempted to study. She cleared the small dining room table and set up her books, folders and study notes. She set her kitchen timer for forty minutes and sat herself down at the table, bending her head industriously to her books. She conscientiously read for five minutes, wielding her highlighter pen – the lazy person's way of making notes, she had always thought. After five more minutes she slumped back in her chair. Nothing was going in; nothing. She might as well be reading Swahili for all the sense it was making.

Kate got up and made herself a cup of tea. You're just tired, she told herself; but she knew it was more than that. It was Miller, long-lost to his family. It was Trixie, vibrant and beautiful and loved, and that still not being enough to save her. It was Olbeck, because just what the hell was going on with him and why hadn't he confided in her? It was Anderton and the sudden air of mystery that now surrounded him. It was Andrew Stanton, who'd loved her; why hadn't she loved him? What the hell was wrong with her? I'm alone, thought Kate, staring blankly ahead of her. If I died here, tonight, how long would it be before someone noticed?

She told herself to stop being ridiculous. Of course someone would notice. She tipped the cold cup of tea down the sink and tried again to concentrate on her studies. *I'm alone*. The thought kept recurring, like some kind of mordant song reverberating around her head. In the end, in utter frustration, she slammed the text book shut and gave up and went to bed, to stare up at the ceiling, trying not to listen to the two-word sentence that kept repeating in her head.

Chapter Seven

JOHN HENRY MILLER'S FUNERAL TOOK place on the following day. Kate dressed in a black suit and stopped on route to buy a small bunch of white roses. As she pocketed her change, she wondered why she was making the effort. Miller had been a vagrant, a petty criminal, a drug addict. Perhaps he'd caused harm to someone, even serious harm. Why was she doing this? We've all caused harm to someone, she reminded herself as she drove towards the crematorium.

It was a shabby little place; the entrance hall, with a swirly-patterned carpet, clearly hadn't been redecorated since the late seventies. Kate took a seat in the small hall and was unsurprised to see that, apart from the person conducting the service, she was the only one there. The pang that the realisation gave her took her by surprise. She found herself blinking hard as the vicar began the words of the service. She observed the coffin, which lay at the front of the room, and with another sharp pang saw that it was the first coffin she'd ever seen which looked too big. At every other funeral she'd ever been to, the coffin always looked too small, but this one was the opposite. It was because Kate could recall just how pathetic the remains it held were, how diminished, how reduced.

The vicar paused for a moment, and in the silence that followed, Kate heard footsteps behind her, the ring of high heels on the linoleum floor of the chapel. She turned and was astonished to see someone else taking a seat at the back of the room; a teenage girl, very young, barely sixteen. She was dressed top to toe in black, with her long hair piled up on top of her head and her eyes heavily outlined in kohl. Kate blinked. Was she John Miller's daughter? A granddaughter, even? The girl caught her gaze and quickly looked down at the floor. Kate turned back to face the front of the room as the vicar resumed his short speech, her curiosity piqued.

Once the ceremony was over and the too-big coffin had disappeared behind a pair of faded purple curtains, the vicar nodded at Kate and then left by a side door. Kate hurried to intercept the teenage girl, who was moving quite slowly towards the main entrance in her high heels.

"Hello," said Kate as she reached her side. As soon as she did so, she recognised the girl. It was the girl who, along with her teenage boyfriend, had actually found Miller's body. Kate was so flabbergasted that for a moment she stopped walking. The girl walked on, her head bowed. Kate quickly caught up with her again. "Thanks for coming," she said. Then, just to be sure, she asked, "It's Mia, isn't it?"

Mia nodded. "Yes."

She hadn't stopped walking, although her pace had slowed. Kate hesitated for a moment, unsure of what to ask. "Did you – did you *know* Mr. Miller?" she demanded. Surely that had to be too much of a coincidence?

Mia shook her head. "No. No, I didn't. I just – I wanted to come because – well, I just couldn't stand the thought of no one being here, and I thought that's what might happen. Because he didn't have anyone, did he? He was all alone."

All of a sudden, Kate found herself absurdly near to tears. It was the thought of this young girl – this *child* – being so sensitive, so decent, to want to give a total stranger a dignified goodbye. If that didn't warm your heart, nothing would.

"That was very good of you, Mia," she said, when she was able to speak. "Very good and kind of you."

Mia half-smiled. "It's awful to think that no one would miss you, isn't it?"

"Yes, it is," Kate said honestly. "It's very sad. How did you know where to come?"

They had reached the driveway in front of the chapel now and a blast of wintry air caught them both unawares. Mia clutched her black jacket to her neck, shivering. "The lady – the officer who talked to us afterwards – she rang up and told me."

Kate nodded. "How have you been, anyway?"

"I'm okay." Mia said it in a stout sort of way that made Kate smile inwardly. "Olly's not doing too good."

"I'm sorry to hear that," said Kate, unsurprised. You didn't fall into a decomposed body – literally – and expect to brush that off lightly. "Is he having counselling? Are you?"

They made small talk for a few more minutes before the cold wind forced them to say goodbye. Kate watched Mia walk off towards the bus stop. When she walked back to her car and drove off, she felt a little bit better about things. Not much, but a bit.

Chapter Eight

THE FINE WEATHER RETURNED THE next day. Kate drove through a golden morning, the leaves on the trees seeming to absorb and send back the rays of the sun, shining out in tints of red, amber and chestnut. The roads were fairly clear and Kate enjoyed her drive so much it was almost with regret that she drew up outside Kyla Mellor's house and parked the car.

It was a large house, but much newer than the Arlens' rambling old farmhouse. Almost aggressively modern, the outside was mostly cedar cladding, tinted glass and blocks of stone. Kate looked around, taking in the landscaped gardens, the covered swimming pool and the expensive sports car parked carelessly on the gravel drive. Plenty of money here, but that was true of most of the neighbourhood wasn't it? Did Kyla even work?

Kate rang the bell and a second later the door was pulled open by Kyla, who had obviously been watching for her approach. She was dressed in a navy and white striped top and dark blue skinny jeans, and Kate, who never worried about her weight, felt quite chubby next to her. Kyla's long blonde hair was pulled up into a messy ponytail and she had the kind of effortless style that Kate associated with those who had modelled for a living. She chanced a guess and asked if that was what Kyla did.

Kyla smiled a rather embarrassed smile. "How did you know that? I used to be a model. I haven't done anything since Gaia was born."

Kate managed not to guffaw at the name. "Gaia's your daughter? How old is she?"

Kyla's smile fell away. "Two and a half, almost the same age as Manon. Trixie and I met at an NCT class."

What was the NCT? Kate tried to look as though she knew. She had come prepared to dig a little into Kyla's relationship with Trixie, but she realised that it might be more worthwhile to let Kyla talk naturally about her friend. However Kate had thought that Kyla might be more of a natural talker than she was turning out to be.

Kyla made coffee, which was lukewarm and too weak. Kate took one sip and abandoned it. "Would you say you and Trixie were close friends?" she asked.

Kyla's gaze flickered then dropped to her coffee cup. She hadn't drunk much of it either. "I suppose so."

"Would she confide in you? If she had any worries or problems?"

Kyla was still looking down. "I guess so."

This was frustrating. Kate knew that Kyla was holding something back, but what? Was it important? "Were you aware that Trixie took drugs?"

"No," Kyla said, too quickly and too loudly. "I was horrified when I found out. I couldn't believe it."

"Hmm," Kate said and watched the other woman flush. "So you never took drugs with Trixie?"

"No!"

"Never?"

"I told you, no. I don't do drugs. Particularly not when I'm around my *children*." Kyla's high cheekbones were stained with red, but Kate wasn't sure if it was with anger or embarrassment. "Trixie and I used to have a drink together sometimes, when the kids were in bed. That was all."

"Okay," said Kate.

Kyla noticed her still-full cup. "You haven't touched your coffee. Shall I make you another?"

"No thanks," said Kate quickly. "I'm sorry if these questions are upsetting you, Mrs. Mellor, but it's useful for me to find out more about Trixie – from the people who knew her best."

Kyla was looking down at the table again, her face serious. She nodded, her blonde fringe catching on her eyelashes.

Kate pressed on, taking advantage of the silence. "Would you say that Trixie was happily married?" she asked.

Kyla looked astonished, then embarrassed. "I – I don't know. I think so. Well, I'm not sure."

"Can you elaborate?"

Kyla looked as though she was regretting saying anything. "Oh, I don't know. She used to tell me when she and Jake had had a row, now and again. But that's normal in a marriage, isn't it?"

"So you don't think she and Mr. Arlen were having any kind of marriage difficulties or anything like that?"

"No. No, I don't think so."

Kate pondered, wondering where to go next. Kyla got up and cleared their full cups away, putting them down on the kitchen counter near the sink. Kate watched her, just for something to do, and realised that Kyla's hands were trembling. She looked closer. Yes, they were shaking. Kyla was either terrified or she was badly hung over. Kate didn't think it was that – there was no smell of stale alcohol around her and she looked great, glowing skin and clear eyes. So why was she so nervous?

"Mrs. Mellor, can I ask you if you've got something to tell me?" asked Kate, taking the bull by the horns.

Kyla threw her a quick, nervous glance. "What do you mean?"

"Is there anything you want to tell me?" That was always an effective question. It was amazing how people spilled the beans if they thought you already knew something.

It didn't appear to work on Kyla; she had closed herself off. Kate could see her face become blank, smoothing into a neutral expression. "No," said Kyla. "I don't have anything to tell you, other than what I've already said."

"Can I ask you your whereabouts on the night Trixie died?"

That red stain once again graced Kyla's sharp cheekbones. "Why do you need to know?"

"It's standard procedure, Mrs. Mellor. I'm not accusing you of anything. Where were you on the night Trixie died?"

"I was here. At home."

Kate nodded. "Can anyone confirm that? Your husband, perhaps?"

Kyla looked away. "No, he wasn't here. He was working abroad all of last week."

"Did you talk to anyone on the phone at all? Use social media?"

"I don't do social media. I think I might have spoken to my mother early in the evening. She rang about dinner time."

DRIVING AWAY AFTER THE INTERVIEW had concluded, Kate found herself tapping the steering wheel lightly with irritation. That woman knew something. Was it possible that she was the person who'd been with Trixie the night she died? Kate considered the idea and then dismissed it. She wasn't sure she believed Kyla when she'd said she'd had no idea that Trixie took drugs, but she had sounded a lot more convincing when she'd said she herself didn't take them. Of course, being a former model, she'd probably partaken in the past, but that wasn't to say that she still indulged. Kate shook her head, irritated with herself. This was all hot air, conjecture, supposition. She made a mental note to check whether the tests on the drugs found in Trixie Arlen's bed had come back with results. Then, at least, she'd know what they were dealing with.

Chapter Nine

THAT NIGHT, KATE BENT TO her books again and felt a little better about her chances of passing the exam. It's not the end of the world if I don't, she told herself as she sipped camomile tea and made careful notes on one of her many lined note pads. I can always retake them. But the humiliation of failing... Kate didn't *fail* at things. Relationships, yes; but never *work* things. She took a deep breath and tried to focus back on the text that was blurring before her tired eyes.

She called it a day at midnight and went straight to bed, not stopping to shower as she normally did at the end of the day. Despite all her anxieties, she passed a dreamless night and awoke refreshed the next morning. So much so that when her phone rang before she'd even switched on the kettle, she managed not to groan. It was Olbeck.

"Fancy coming with me to re-interview Arlen?" he asked. Kate could hear traffic noise faintly in the background and hoped he was using the hands-free if he was driving.

"I thought you and Anderton were doing that?"

"He's bailed on me. Something about a meeting back at the station. Will you come?"

"Of course," said Kate, pleased to be asked. She flew around getting ready and was waiting on the doorstep, bag in hand, when Olbeck pulled his car into the kerb outside her house.

"By the way, Jeff says can you do the night of the fourteenth for dinner?"

"That's my exam day," said Kate. She felt another jump of anxiety and vowed that she would spend the whole of the evening studying, no matter how tired she was after work.

"Oh," said Olbeck. "Right. No matter. We'll do it another time."

"Actually," said Kate, thinking aloud. "I'd like to come over. It'll be something to look forward to after the horrors of the day."

Olbeck grinned. "That's the spirit. Great – that's settled then. Dinner at ours on the fourteenth." He seemed about to say something else, but clearly changed his mind. Kate was aware of the sense of suppressed excitement that she'd noticed before. She opened her mouth to ask him outright and then closed it again. If he wanted to tell her, he would.

The crowd of paparazzi at the Arlens' farmhouse had depleted to a solitary car parked by the entrance gate, with a man leaning disconsolately against the bonnet, a camera dangling from his hand. He perked up a little as Olbeck drove closer and indicated for the farmhouse lane but slumped when he realised that the car didn't contain anyone famous. He still took a few shots of them as they drove past him. Kate fought the urge to give him the finger as they went by.

"Paparazzi have thinned out a bit," remarked Olbeck as they drove nearer the farmhouse, stating the obvious.

"A week's a long time in show business," said Kate.

"Wait until the funeral next week. You can imagine what that's going to be like."

Kate made a noise of agreement. She thought of the thronging crowds that would no doubt be there, the famous names and faces, the attendant media, the footage that would no doubt make it onto the BBC. What a contrast it would be to the funeral of John Miller. Yet Trixie and John had died of the same thing, disparate as their lives had been. It was strange.

"It's so strange," she muttered to herself.

"What is?" asked Olbeck.

Kate shook herself back to reality. "Oh, nothing."

OLBECK PARKED THE CAR NEXT to the black Range Rover that had been parked there on their previous visit. Jacob Arlen opened the farmhouse door before they'd even locked the car and stood on the doorstep, as if guarding it, his arms hugged across his body. He was dressed in a sombre grey suit and looked much older than he had on the day he'd found his wife's body.

"The children are still with my parents," he said as the officers approached him. "I didn't want to talk with them around."

Did that mean he had something significant to impart? Kate wondered as she followed Arlen and Olbeck through to the kitchen. Possibly not. She would have to wait and see.

Arlen didn't offer them any refreshments. Kate imagined that he had an assistant who took care of that side of things in his office, and he didn't look like the kind of man who knew his way around his own kitchen. He sat down in the chair at the head of the table too quickly, as if the strength had left his body without warning.

Olbeck always started this type of interview with an expression of condolence. Arlen didn't say anything but nodded almost impatiently, as if wanting to dispense with the pleasantries and get straight down to business.

Olbeck didn't beat around the bush. "Were you aware that your wife was taking heroin, Mr. Arlen?"

Arlen visibly winced. He was silent for a long moment and then said slowly, as if the words were being pulled out of him, "I was – I became aware that she was doing that."

"How long have you known?"

"Not long. A matter of months, if that."

"It didn't worry you?"

Arlen looked up, incredulous. "Are you insane? Of course it worried me. It worried me *sick*. When I found out she was using again, I – I – she swore it was a one-off. That she'd just got so bored being at home all the time, that it was an impulse thing."

Trixie Arlen took heroin on impulse? Kate tried not to let her scepticism show. That was a lie, but was it Trixie's or Arlen's?

Olbeck probed Arlen for more details. "You first found out she'd taken heroin when, exactly?"

Arlen briefly closed his eyes, as if in pain. "It was a couple of months ago. Things hadn't been – we hadn't been getting on very well, and I'd been away a lot. I found a box of syringes at the back of her bedside table drawer and an empty plastic bag." He looked away. "She swore blind it was a one-off."

"Did you believe her?" asked Olbeck.

"I don't know," Arlen replied, again slowly and painfully. "I wanted to believe her. I hadn't ever known her when she was – was involved in that kind of world. Trixie said that when Ivo – her first husband – died, she never touched the stuff again. Ever."

"So why would she start using it again, do you think?"

Arlen was shaking his head. "I don't actually know that she *was* using it again. Not regularly." He paused and his brows drew down in a frown. "I searched the bedroom a couple of times. I didn't tell her that's what I was doing. But I didn't find anything."

Probably because Trixie had got better at hiding it, Kate thought but didn't say. Was it likely that Trixie had told the truth? The reality was that she had taken heroin again at least once more – the night she died. But had there been other times?

Arlen was still speaking. "A couple of times I came home and she was – well, there was just something a little off about her. She didn't really drink much but it was sometimes as if she was, well, a little drunk. But I couldn't smell it on her or anything like that." He looked directly at Kate. "I was worried, very worried, because she was on her own a lot with the children."

"Did you address this with her again at any time?" Kate asked.

Arlen's gaze dropped to the table. "There wasn't really anything I could say. I couldn't find anything to actually accuse her of."

"Did any of Trixie's friends, like Kyla Mellors for example, ever mention any concerns to you?"

Arlen's eyelids flickered minutely. He cleared

his throat. "No, not that I can recall. No one said anything to me."

There was a hint – just a hint – of evasiveness in his reply. Kate frowned, wondering whether to take him up on it. But even as she was wondering, Olbeck asked Arlen something else, moving on to another subject.

"We've eliminated most of the fingerprints that our scientists found in the bedroom, Mr. Arlen. There's one though that you might be able to help us with."

Arlen looked faintly alarmed. "I would?"

Olbeck gave him the rundown from the fingerprint report. "So you can see, it's this unknown female we're looking for. Would Trixie's friends ever go up to your bedroom?"

Arlen's cheeks were faintly mottled. "That's rather presumptuous, Detective Inspector, isn't it? What are you implying?" Before Olbeck could answer, Arlen's face suddenly cleared and he went from looking mortified to looking relieved. "I'm sorry, how stupid of me. I didn't even think – it's almost certainly our cleaner. Rosa. She comes in every week."

Of course the Arlens would have had a cleaner, thought Kate. No doubt a gardener too, a dog-walker, an ironing service. It was only surprising that there hadn't been a nanny, but that particular bit of domesticity hadn't appear to have been outsourced. Again, Kate found herself doubting the evidence of her own eyes. Was it really likely that Trixie Arlen, earth mother and domestic goddess, would have risked being under the influence of a class A drug when she had the responsibility of three small children? Wasn't it more likely that someone – some unknown someone – had forced her to inject herself? But why? What possible motive would there be?

Olbeck asked Arlen for Rosa's details. Kate could have advised him to save his breath; there was no way that a man like Arlen would have been involved in hiring or supervising a domestic servant when even making coffee for visitors appeared beyond him.

As expected, Arlen didn't have a clue where Rosa lived, what her surname was, or even if she worked for an agency.

"Would you expect her to come to work again?" asked Kate quickly. "Considering what's happened? When does she normally come here?"

Arlen looked more confused than the simple question warranted. "I'm not sure. I was never really here when she was here. Wait a moment—" He got up and walked over to a noticeboard, thickly plastered with children's drawings, takeaway leaflets, school notices and business cards, on the opposite wall. He peered at it more closely and then carefully pulled a drawing pin free. Several other pieces of paper fell to the floor but he didn't bother to pick them up. "Here you are," he said, handing the little card to Kate. I knew I'd seen something before – that's the agency Rosa comes from, I think."

"Thank you, Mr. Arlen," said Kate, who looked at it briefly before tucking it away in her bag. It was pink, with the logo of the company in a flowery black script spelling out *Home Angels, Domestic Cleaning*. "It will be very useful to be able to eliminate another person from our enquiries."

Jacob Arlen nodded, looking serious. Kate glanced at Olbeck, wondering if he was going to bring up the most serious point of the interview. He gave her a minute nod, tacit permission to go ahead.

"There's something else that we need to discuss with you, Mr. Arlen," Kate said. "As far as we're aware, bearing in mind we're still waiting for the results of the toxicology tests, it seems fairly clear that your wife died of an overdose of diacetylmorphine – heroin, in other words." Arlen was watching her face intently, utterly focused on her words. Kate continued. "The problem is that despite that, we found no drugs, no drugs paraphernalia, no syringes, nothing at all with your wife's body."

There was a moment of silence. Kate watched Arlen's expression keenly. She could have sworn that the revelation came as an utter surprise to him.

"My God," Arlen said softly. "How - how is that possible?"

Kate cleared her throat before she spoke again. "It's possible, Mr. Arlen, because someone removed all evidence of drug use from the scene."

"What are you saying? It couldn't – Trixie couldn't have moved it, hidden it or whatever before – before she died?"

Both Kate and Olbeck had considered that possibility. They'd had the benefit of advice from Doctor Telling on the likelihood of just that happening. Kate explained to Arlen what Doctor Telling had told them.

"I'm afraid not. Your wife would have died very quickly after the injection – a matter of minutes. She wouldn't have been physically able to move far, let alone go to the trouble of hiding drugs and syringes in a place where we've not been able to find them."

Arlen's head had lowered and he was staring at the table again. "That means there was someone else here with Trixie. Doesn't it?" he concluded, looking up at them both. "Do you know who?"

"Our enquiries are continuing," Olbeck replied. "But there's another possibility, Mr. Arlen."

"There is?"

Kate and Olbeck exchanged glances. If this guy was lying, he was pretty good. "You could have removed whatever was there yourself, Mr Arlen," said Kate. She paused for a moment to let it sink in, watching Arlen's eyes widen with shock, and then went in for the kill. "Did you?"

"No!" Arlen sat back in his chair, looking from one face to another, wide-eyed. "I had no idea – I didn't see anything. Why would I do that?"

"I don't know, Mr. Arlen," Kate said mildly. "Perhaps you were worried about your wife's reputation. You didn't want it known that she'd died of a drug overdose. Perhaps you were worried that your children would come into the room and get hold of whatever was lying around."

Arlen raised a shaking hand to his temple. He was breathing quickly but Kate could see that he was gradually regaining self-control. "I touched nothing, I saw nothing," he said and his voice was quite firm. "You have to believe me. I can't prove it, but I promise you I didn't see anything like that. There wasn't anything like that. And I—" He stopped speaking abruptly.

"Yes?" prompted Kate after a moment's silence.

Arlen dropped his hand back to his lap, limply, as if all the strength had run out of his arm. "I looked," he said simply. "After I realised she was dead. I think I – I think I knew why she'd died, because of the drugs."

Olbeck leaned forward. "You suspected your wife had died of a drugs overdose?"

"I didn't *know*. I just – after I'd caught her that

117

last time... I suspected, that was all. But I promise you this, there was nothing there. I looked around – not very well, I was too shaken up and I knew I had to call an ambulance and stop the kids from seeing her – but I had a quick look under the bed and on the dressing table. There was nothing like that there. No syringes or anything." He looked at them both again and his words had the simple ring of truth. "I found nothing. I saw nothing."

"Very well, Mr. Arlen," Olbeck said. "We'll need to amend your statement with words to that effect."

"Yes." Arlen slumped back against his chair, putting his head back and closing his eyes. "Yes, I understand that."

"Do you have any idea who this person who was with your wife on the night she died might be?"

"I have absolutely no idea.""

"It wouldn't have been a friend of hers? Of yours?"

"I can't imagine so. I can't imagine any of our friends being caught up in – in that kind of thing."

"Can you give me a list of your wife's close friends?" asked Kate. "We'll need to talk to them. We've already interviewed Mrs. Mellors but—"

"Oh, it wouldn't have been Kyla," said Arlen, quickly. "She would never do anything like that."

Kate paused. There was something – God, what was it? – in Arlen's tone. Something not quite natural. "You know Mrs. Mellors well, then?" she asked, casually.

When he answered her, Arlen sounded as normal as he ever had. "Yes, very well. She and Trixie and I are good friends. I play golf with her husband sometimes, too."

Kate wondered whether she'd imagined that brief flicker of strangeness in Arlen's voice. It was sometimes too easy to see undercurrents, to see something that wasn't there. She filed the thought away in her head for later perusal.

Arlen scribbled several names down on a sheet of paper, pausing and frowning over each one, before passing it to Kate. She glanced down at the list of five names and rough addresses and sighed at the thought of the time it would take to interview all five women. Still, it had to be done. After making an appointment with Arlen to amend his statement in Abbeyford the next day, they took their leave.

"So what did you think?" Olbeck asked as they drove away. He gave the solitary paparazzi a cheery wave as they drove by him onto the main road. The man scowled and Kate bit back a giggle.

"What did *you* think?" she countered.

Olbeck glanced over at her. "I think he's hiding something."

Kate felt a leap of gladness. It hadn't been her imagination, then. "So do I, funnily enough."

"I don't mean about the drugs," Olbeck went on, flicking on the indicator as they left the village and joined the bypass. "I actually think he's being totally truthful about that. He didn't see anything by Trixie's body that morning because there wasn't anything there to see."

"Yes. I agree." Kate watched the trees on the embankment of the dual carriageway flash by. The leaves were hitting the peak of their autumn colours; a kaleidoscope of copper, amber and auburn splendour. "So what *is* he hiding?"

"God knows. Everyone's always hiding *something* in a case like this. But is it significant or isn't it?"

"I'll do some checking," said Kate slowly, thinking it through. "Work out the timings for what he says he was doing that morning and the night before." Too late, she remembered they hadn't questioned Arlen about the bruising on his wife's arm and cursed. "That was slack of us, Mark," she said, explaining when he looked over enquiringly. "Too much going on at the moment."

"Tell me about it," Olbeck said with feeling. "Anyway, let me know about Arlen. Can you and Theo take the interviews with Trixie's friends?"

"Yep," said Kate, watching as the houses of Abbeyford began to roll into view. "I'm going to see how many stupid children's names I can gather at the same time."

She was rewarded with Olbeck's laugh at they drew into the forecourt of the police station, and she smiled as she bent to retrieve her handbag from the footwell.

Chapter Ten

TRUE TO HER WORD, KATE began interviewing
Trixie Arlen's friends the next morning. She and
Theo drove down together and worked their way
through the list methodically. Kate had anticipated
being unable to get hold of several of the people
listed – she'd thought that most of them would be
at work – but that turned out not to be the case.
The five names on the list – Francesca Bolton, Sian
Hills, Veronica Tibbert-Jones, Melinda D'Agnew
and Carla Denford – all turned out to be women who
looked as if they'd emerged from the same cloning
laboratory, or perhaps a factory. All five were tall,
thin, and well-groomed: all with that indefinable
air of polish that only significant amounts of
money and equally significant amounts of free time
can achieve. Kate, who normally thought she was
doing all right, considering how little time she had
to spend on her appearance, felt positively scruffy
next to them all. Theo, on the other hand, looked as
though all his Christmases had come at once.

Not a single one of the five worked outside the home, as far as Kate could ascertain. Melinda D'Agnew did announce proudly that she was starting up her own business – one that Kate dismissively referred to in the privacy of her own head as a 'cupcake-bunting business'. In Kate's eyes, it was clearly a tax fiddle, on behalf of Melinda's husband, but she kept her mouth shut and made appropriate interested noises.

The five women were so alike that Kate had to keep referring back to her notes to see which of them they'd already talked to – she was beginning to get confused. It didn't help that they all looked the same – a mane of long, glossy hair, discreet makeup, all wearing the same unofficial uniform of a striped Breton top and dark, close-fitting jeans. What made it more frustrating was that none of them had anything interesting to tell Kate and Theo at all.

"No, Trixie was fine, she was completely normal last time I saw her," said Francesca Bolton, pouring coffee into fine white china cups. "There wasn't anything worrying her as far as I could tell."

"Trixie and Jacob seemed fine to me." Sian Hills offered them herbal tea and some sort of desiccated 'artisanal' biscuit. "They had their ups and downs of course, like anyone. But I'm sure there was nothing really bad going on in their relationship."

"Trixie? Take drugs? Oh no, you've got to

be kidding. Seriously, like, she would never do something like that. God, it's so – so *sad*, isn't it, doing drugs? No one does that anymore." Veronica Tibbert-Jones ran a hand through the long, shiny sweep of her hair, scoffing. "She liked a drink, of course. Wine o'clock and all that. But heroin? Oh my God, no. I can't believe *that*."

Melinda D'Agnew gave Kate and Theo freshly squeezed orange juice. Kate watched her long, slim hands and finely polished nails and wondered just how much, if any, housework Melinda did. "Trixie and I would talk, of course we would. But she didn't mention anything to me that I thought was odd. We talked about business of course – I used to pump her for tips, given she was so successful. She was very generous, you know. A very warm heart. A really genuine person."

By the time Kate and Theo got to Carla Denford, Kate felt as though she'd been talking to identikit Sloanes for most of her adult life. Carla Denford opened the front door to her large, expensive house and Kate bit back a scream of frustration, realising that Carla was, yes, dressed in a navy striped top, grey skinny jeans and had a fall of long, glossy hair. They followed her into the large dining room-cum-play area at the back of the house and Kate braced herself for the offer of more healthy hot drinks.

"Want a drink?" asked Carla. "G and T do you?"

Kate blinked. It was twelve thirty in the

afternoon. "No thanks, Mrs. Denford," she replied, glaring at Theo, who looked as if he were about to accept. He shut his mouth hastily.

"Because I get so fed up of fucking *tea*," said Carla with surprisingly bitterness and moved to the enormous SMEG fridge.

Hastily, Kate consulted her list of questions and chose one at random. "How well did you know Trixie Arlen, Mrs. Denford?"

"About as well as I know anyone else here," said Carla, sitting down with a brimming glass. She took a long, thirsty gulp and put it down with a sigh. "Which is to say not at all."

"How do you mean?" Kate realised Carla had probably had one or two drinks already, although her speech was clear enough.

"It's all surface, here," said Carla. Her head drooped towards the table and she put a finger in a spilled droplet on the kitchen table, smearing it in a circle. "The men all work in London in ridiculously well-paid jobs, and the women sit at home in their lovely designer houses, outsourcing their childcare. It's so bloody *boring*; I could just scream sometimes. Instead, well, I..." she gestured to her glass and made a shrugging gesture which was both eloquent and sad.

Kate gave Theo a meaningful glance and, for once, he understood and got up, muttering something about getting something from the car. Once he was out of the room, Kate put down her notebook and leant forward a little, mirroring Carla's position.

"So, it's a bit shit, is it?" Kate said, in a tone she hoped was both wry and sympathetic.

Carla looked at her gratefully. "Oh God, you have no idea. It's funny though, because Trixie was the only one who – she was a bit different. She had a *spark*. A bit of life. At least she'd actually *done* something with her life – before, I mean."

"You said you didn't know her well. Did she ever confide in you?"

"Not really. It was more – I guess I confided in her, more than the other way round. We met at an NCT class—"

"Yes, what *is* that?" asked Kate, unable to help herself.

Carla gave her a slightly odd look. "National Childbirth Trust."

"Oh, right. Thanks."

"Yeah, anyway, we met at the NCT class, caught up with each other a few times after our babies were born—"

"What's your baby's name?" asked Kate, unable to help herself again.

Again, Carla looked slightly surprised. "James."

"Oh, that's *lovely*," said Kate fervently. She got a grip on herself. "So you met up quite frequently after you had your children?"

"Sort of. Occasionally I went to her house or she

came here. What they call a 'playdate', around here, which is *ridiculous* because the babies couldn't care less about playing with other babies. Anyway, we did see each other a bit."

"Did Trixie ever seem worried about anything to you? Anxious about anything?"

Carla fell silent, twirling her almost empty glass around in her hand. She appeared to be thinking hard. "There's one thing she said once that I thought was strange," she said, slowly. "It stuck with me."

"What was that?" prompted Kate.

"We were in the kitchen at her place, just chatting, and the radio was on. There was something in the news about – oh, God, what was it? – oh yes, that's right, about a mother who'd been found not guilty of killing her baby. God, *horrible*. Anyway, I said something about not understanding how anyone could do that and Trixie said, in this really sad, slow way, that sometimes people did things that they would always regret, even if they hadn't meant to do them at the time."

Kate paused. "That's it?"

Carla nodded. "Yeah, that was all. She changed the subject the next minute and...I don't know, it was just her voice that got me. Real...real *grief*, kind of dragging through it. It made me shiver."

"She never elaborated on what she meant?"

"No. I remembered it from time to time and thought I'd ask her about it, but I never really felt the time was right. And now I'll never get the chance."

Her voice, finally thickening from alcohol, broke. For a moment, Kate was sure Carla would burst into tears but she seemed to have more self-control than was at first apparent. She took a deep, shaky breath and appeared to compose herself.

There was nothing else that Carla appeared to be able to tell her. Kate eventually gave her thanks and said goodbye. She wanted to say something kind, something that would make Carla feel better, but she couldn't think what. 'Go back to London' was probably not something that would make Carla feel better at all. So Kate said nothing, and smiled and thanked her, and Carla, red-eyed and faintly swaying, just nodded and closed the door behind her in silence.

"Blimey," said Theo as they drove away, Kate taking the wheel for the homeward journey. "Some people don't know they're born, eh? All that money, expensive cars, designer goods and she's still a miserable cow."

"Oh, for God's sake," said Kate, more crossly than she'd intended. "It's not about *money*. Carla's clearly an intelligent woman who feels like a complete outsider here. She's unhappy because she's lonely and bored, that's all."

"Yeah, right," said Theo, looking unconvinced.

"Well, I think that's what's the matter with her,"

said Kate, more gently. She felt like adding 'I know how she feels', but didn't. What she did ponder aloud was the question, "I wonder if Trixie Arlen felt like Carla did? I wonder that very much."

"Would explain why she was chasing the dragon again," said Theo.

"I think that's *smoking* heroin," said Kate. "Not injecting it. But I see your point." She remembered that she had an appointment with the drug and alcohol counsellor the next day. And the day after that was exam day. She swallowed, queasily. Out loud she said, "Wonder if Arlen's given his new statement yet?"

"Don't know," said Theo, yawning. He settled his head back comfortably against the headrest. "Wake me up when we get back to Abbeyford. Those chicks have worn me out."

"I never thought I'd hear that coming from you," Kate joked. Theo said nothing but smiled lazily as the car joined the dual carriageway that would take them back to their home town.

Chapter Eleven

THE NEXT DAY STARTED BADLY. Kate woke late, after staying up until the early hours trying to cram more knowledge into her head, staring at her notes until they blurred before her. She wasn't sure it had done much good. She was in too much of a rush to have breakfast before she left the house and had to stop off at a service station to grab a cup of coffee and a greasy sausage roll to tide her over.

The sat nav took her into Charlock, the neighbouring suburb to Arbuthon Green, to the modern brick building housing Outreach, the drug rehabilitation service provider. She was due to meet one of the counsellors, Jason Neville, and made the appointment with a minute to spare. Neville turned out to be a man of around Kate's age, with very pale blue eyes and the white skin of a natural redhead. His fox-coloured hair was curly and worn long, tied back into a pony tail. He had the warm, approachable demeanour typical to professional counsellors.

Kate sat opposite him in an office so messy it looked as though it had been burgled. Kate had actually never been in a counsellor's office that was any different; it seemed to go with the job. God knew how they ever found anything. Perhaps there was hidden order amongst the chaos. She turned her eyes from the mountainous piles of paperwork, empty mugs and crumpled food containers on Jason Neville's desk and focused her attention on what he was saying.

"We see all sorts of people here, Detective Sergeant," he said, fiddling with one of the folders on his desk. As he did so, a teetering pile of paper crashed to the floor. "Oh, bugger. Sorry." He began picking them up. Kate bent to help him but he said quickly, "Oh, I'm sorry, these are all confidential. Please don't bother."

Kate could have given him the 'nothing's confidential in a murder case', but she didn't; firstly because they weren't sure whether this *was* a murder case, and secondly, she didn't want to antagonise him. She wanted Mr. Neville to open up as much as he was able to.

"So you see all sorts of people?" Kate prompted, once the papers were returned to even more glorious disorder on the man's desk.

Her eyes fell on a leaflet entitled *Is Your Child a Drug Addict?* In smaller type beneath the flaring headline was a box containing several bullet points.

Kate read the first few before she had to bring her gaze back up to Neville's face. *Possible signs of heroin addiction: constricted (small) pupils, noticeable needle 'track marks', hyper-alertness followed by sudden sleepiness...*

Jason Neville was already answering. "That's right. I know there's the public stereotype of an addict – certainly that of an alcoholic – but that's the stereotype, not the reality."

"I'm interested in your clients who are heroin addicts. Would you say they range in type? I know you can't tell me specifics—" she added quickly as he began to frown, "but it would be really helpful to have some sort of guidance."

"Right. Well, we've got people in addiction therapy here from all walks of life. Housewives, builders, professionals. Doctors." He hesitated and then added. "Even a police officer."

Kate was predictably agog. Who was it? Surely not anyone she knew? She filed that thought away for later and merely raised her eyebrows at Neville, who looked at her with a slight touch of defiance, ready to block the questions that he seemed to anticipate coming his way.

When Kate remained silent, he cleared his throat and continued speaking. "We work on a combination of therapies here. We run a methadone clinic, we have several medical treatments that clients can access if we feel it would be appropriate for them. The bulk of our work, though, is psychotherapy."

"I see. Is it the case that most of your patients are dealing with some kind of life trauma – that they're self-medicating with drugs to treat that?"

Neville shrugged. "Sometimes. Quite often they're working through horrendous childhoods, deep-seated emotional abuse, physical abuse, that sort of thing. Or they're unhappy because of something terrible that's happened to them in adult life – a bereavement or a bad accident. Quite a few people self-medicate, as you say, with heroin because it's such an effective pain-killer. Obviously you know that it's a derivative of morphine, which has a wide-spread legitimate use in our hospitals and surgeries."

"Yes, I'm aware of that," Kate said patiently. Briefly, she thought of her mother and how her drinking had blighted Kate's life from childhood. What was her mother dealing with, what trauma from the past was she fighting? Kate's oldest brother had died young, almost too early for Kate to have any memory of him; had that been what started her mother on the slippery slope to self-destruction? Was it something other than that, something earlier and never spoken of in her mother's life? For a moment, Kate wanted nothing more than to run from Jason Neville's room and drive at full speed to her mother's house; she wanted to run through the front doorway and fling her arms about her mother. How long had it been since they last talked? Four years? More?

With an effort, Kate brought her attention back to the present and to what Jason Neville was saying. He was fidgeting with a mug this time and Kate prayed that he wouldn't dislodge another tsunami of paper.

Neville was still speaking. "Of course, once people reach a certain...tipping point, I suppose you'd call it, the problems they're dealing with are all to do with the drug that they're consuming. They behave terribly because they're taking drugs, and then they feel so bad that they have to take more drugs to block out what they've done, and so the cycle just perpetuates. Once we manage to get them into therapy we work very hard on breaking that cycle."

"Yes, I see," said Kate. "What's your success rate?"

"Sorry?"

"Do you have a lot of people who relapse?"

"Yes. Oh, sadly, yes, we do. But then we also have a lot of people who conquer their addictions and go on to live very happy and successful lives."

Kate thought about how to pose the next question. "Would you say that you have clients who might have been clean for years, decades even, and then for one reason or another they go back to using drugs again?"

Jason's pale blue eyes caught her own. There was a long moment of silence. "Yes," he said eventually. "That does happen."

"Why?"

Again he hesitated. "It's difficult to explain, unless you've actually been an addict yourself. There's some research that suggests that once you're addicted to something, you've permanently altered your brain chemistry, and so if you ever begin using again your use spirals out of control very quickly. Whereas a 'normal' person—" he made quotation marks in the air with his fingers, "a normal person can take drugs, even quite regularly, without their use escalating."

Kate frowned. He hadn't actually answered her question. "Yes, I see, but why would someone who's been clean for so long just go back to using drugs again?"

"I don't know," Neville said simply. "Life just gets on top of them. Perhaps they go through another traumatic event. Perhaps they forget just how bad their life was when they were using drugs. Or maybe it's nothing so complicated. Sometimes people just...slip."

LATER, AS KATE DROVE AWAY from the centre, having thanked Jason Neville and made her goodbyes, she found herself thinking of what he had said. What had made Trixie Arlen slip? *Had* she slipped – or was she pushed? Kate reminded herself that they still had to question Jacob Arlen over the bruising on his wife's arm and made a mental note that she would do that tomorrow. Oh God, no, she couldn't tomorrow. Tomorrow was when she would take her exams. Kate swallowed. All thoughts of Trixie Arlen fled, replaced by nerve-grinding anxiety. She wasn't prepared for these exams; she knew she wasn't. Perhaps I should just postpone taking them, she thought to herself, but knew that it would be months before she might get another chance to re-sit them. Months of no career progression. No, no she would take them tomorrow and do her best. Much as she knew that last-minute cramming could be counter-productive, she resolved to spend the evening studying. It'll be fine, she told herself, ignoring the uncoiling worm of uneasiness that writhed in her stomach.

Chapter Twelve

"So how did it go?" asked Theo as Kate slid into the chair of the desk opposite him the next afternoon.

Kate closed her eyes briefly. "Don't ask."

"That bad, eh?" Theo tried to look sympathetic but succeeded only in looking mischievous. "Should have studied harder then, shouldn't you?"

"Shut up!" Kate crashed her chair back from the desk. Theo looked shocked and throughout the office, heads turned. Kate quickly walked to the far side of the room, where the coffee machine was, and made herself a drink with shaking hands, keeping her head down.

The sound of footsteps behind her preceded Theo's quiet apology. "Listen, mate, I'm sorry. I didn't mean to wind you up. Exams are stressful, yeah?"

Kate blinked hard. Theo's apology, on top of the realisation that she really shouldn't have lost her temper in such a childish way, made her feel even worse. "No, I'm sorry," she said, turning round and hoping that her eyes weren't too red. "Sorry. I'm a bit...a bit highly strung, at the moment."

"No worries," said Theo, his cheeky grin bursting out afresh. "Let's have a pint later, yeah? I'm buying."

Kate never drank pints but she appreciated the offer. She returned the grin and they walked back to their desks together. Kate glanced over at Olbeck's office; empty. Never mind, she had dinner with him and Jeff to look forward to tonight, although she hoped she wouldn't have to spend too much time talking about her exams.

They had been as bad as she expected; possibly worse. I've definitely failed, she thought to herself, and the brief lifting of spirits which Theo's kindness provoked flickered and died. She took a gulp of coffee, swallowing past the lump in her throat, and turned her attention to the paperwork littering her desk.

She was halfway through the pile when she came across a copy of Jack Harker's statement about the robbery he'd been victim to. Kate mentally gave herself a shake. It was a measure of her state of mind that she'd almost forgotten that such a thing had happened at all. She made notes to find out if there had been any developments on that case, and whether any more robberies had been reported.

Kate rubbed her temples, feeling overwhelmed. Since her colleague, Rav, had been shot last summer

– thankfully not fatally – the team had been one down, with no replacement for him yet in sight. Kate reminded herself that she had to take that up with Olbeck and Anderton. The extra work occasioned by being short-staffed meant that it was more and more likely mistakes would be made. Look at her and Olbeck, forgetting to ask Arlen about that bruising; it was a rookie error, and unforgiveable in officers of their experience.

Kate sighed and added another thing to the mental list of 'stuff to do' she kept in her head – *call Rav*. It had been several weeks since she'd spoken to him and she wanted to know how he was doing. Rav was supposed to be on long-term sick leave, but Kate wondered whether he'd actually ever want to return. It was a shame; he'd been a good officer, as young as he was.

She jumped as Theo flung himself into his chair, making their desks rock. He had the gleeful expression of someone with some serious gossip to imply. "Well, well, well," he said, taking his time about it. "Now we know why the boss has been so distracted lately."

"What do you mean?" asked Kate.

"Dear, dear," said Theo, ignoring her. "I can see why he *has* been distracted. Ooh-wee...."

"What are you talking about?" Kate said impatiently, but a presentiment of disaster began to filter its way through her. Her heart began to beat a little faster.

Theo finally got to the point. "Anderton's new bird. She's in his office right now. *Hawt!*"

Anderton's new bird. Kate was very aware of her heartbeat now; it rang in her ears like thunder. Her stomach cramped. "What?" she asked, unable to keep her voice steady, but luckily Theo was too busy making lustful noises to notice.

Kate made a mammoth effort and regained control of her voice. "What are you dribbling on about, Theo?" She already knew but she had to hear it again, just to confirm her worst fears.

Theo grinned. "I told you. Anderton's new piece of stuff. She's a lawyer, apparently. Anyway, she's in his office now."

Nobody would ever know what it cost Kate to give a disdainful shrug. "That's nice," she said in a bored tone, keeping her eyes on the screen. She clenched her teeth so hard her jaw hurt as jealousy consumed her. Okay, so she and Anderton had only slept together, once, years ago, but Kate had never given up hope that it would happen again, despite neither of them making any moves towards one another. And now it was too late. Of course it was. You fool, you fool, she told herself fiercely while the blood pounded in her ears and she stared at her computer screen through a mist of tears, utterly unseeing. Why didn't you do something about it when you had the chance? He would have wanted to, you know he would have. What stopped you? Now it's too late. Too late.

She got up abruptly and made her way towards the women's toilets. Her throat was aching with unshed tears. She prayed that no one would be in there, and for once, her prayer was answered. She pushed the button of the hand-dryer and ducked into a cubicle for a few moments, her sobs lost under the roar of hot air. As soon as the dryer switched off, she choked off her tears, biting the back of her hand in an effort to bring herself under control. What a fucking awful day this was turning out to be, she thought. She blotted her face with toilet paper and went out to splash her face at the sink. Luckily she didn't wear much eye-makeup. She made herself stare at the harsh radiance of the overhead strip light in an effort to lessen the redness of her eyes. Then, under control again, she took a deep breath, straightened her back, and left.

She told herself that she would not walk past Anderton's office. She would not. But somehow she found her feet were taking her in that direction, seemingly under no instruction from her brain, as if they'd been bewitched. The blinds in his office were open, and Kate could not have looked away if there'd been a gun to her head. Anderton and a woman were standing quite close together by his desk, laughing about something. The woman was tall and beautiful, with dark blonde hair pulled back into a professional-looking French twist. She wore a very nicely cut pale grey suit and a crisp white shirt, open low at the neck. Kate's bewitched feet slowed and then, as Anderton looked up and their eyes met, Kate found that she could actually walk as fast as she wanted to. She marched back to her desk, her face hot and her heart still pounding as if she had run a race.

SOMEHOW SHE GOT THROUGH THE rest of the afternoon. There was so much to do and nothing she actually wanted to do. Doctor Telling had rung and left her a message asking her to call back when she could, but Kate couldn't quite face doing so, not even for the quiet and soothing tones of the good doctor. I'll do it tomorrow, she told herself, fighting not to put her head in her hands and weep. I'll do it tomorrow when I'm feeling a bit better.

Theo, thank God, kept his mouth shut for most of the afternoon. At about three pm, he muttered something about a hotel – Kate didn't catch the name – and left the office. He hadn't returned by the time Kate was preparing to leave herself; so much for that pint he'd promised her. She hadn't seen Olbeck all afternoon either, but at about six thirty pm, he appeared in the doorway, looked around and saw her, raising his hand.

"Ready for dinner?" he asked, coming over.

Kate nodded. "Can I just ask that we don't mention my exams? At all?"

"Oh dear." Olbeck looked at her sympathetically. "That bad, eh? Never mind. And no, we won't mention them again."

"Thanks."

"I thought I could give you a lift if you like? Save taking two cars."

"Fine, whatever," muttered Kate. She was beginning to feel very tired. It was too much trouble to work out how she was going to get home or how she was going to get to work in the morning. Who cared, anyway?

She was quiet in the car and it took her a while to realise that Olbeck had that strange, suppressed energy about him again. He was fidgeting a little in the driving seat, tapping the foot not on the accelerator, drumming his fingers on the steering wheel. Despite her exhaustion, Kate wondered what was wrong with him and then realised, as she should have before, that he probably had something important to tell her. She felt a pang of anxiety – what if it was bad news? Like what, she asked herself, and then hurried the thought away before she could clarify what she meant. He didn't seem upset, though; the opposite, if anything. Kate opened her mouth to ask him what the matter was and then shut it again. He'll tell me when he's ready, she thought, realising that she was too wrung out and emotional to be able to take it in properly anyway.

In that, she was wrong. Once they were inside Olbeck's house, he ushered her through to the kitchen. Several pans were bubbling on the stove, and there was an open bottle of red wine breathing on the table. Jeff was nowhere to be seen.

Kate looked around for him. "Where's Jeff?"

Olbeck was almost bouncing up and down on his feet. "He just popped out to get something. He'll be back soon." He opened a drawer, stared blindly into it and pushed it shut again. "I should wait for him to be here before I tell you."

Here we go. "Tell me what?" asked Kate, trying to sound enthusiastic.

Olbeck was silent for a moment. "Oh bugger it, I can't wait," he said, grinning. "I've been keeping this in for so long that I think I'll burst if I don't tell you sooner or later. We're getting married."

Married. Olbeck was getting married. Although she felt as though she'd been kicked in the stomach, Kate managed to stretch her lips into a desperate smile.

"That's great—" she began, but Olbeck was still speaking.

"And that's not the best thing. We've been talking about it and we're pretty sure we're going to look into seeing if we can adopt as well!" he said, clasping his hands together in front of his chest.

The room stilled for a moment. Kate felt the smile freeze on her face as that word echoed around her head. *Adopt. We're going to adopt.* There was a moment of sparkling numbness.

"Are you fucking kidding me?" The words came out in a shriek. Kate could feel her face stretched in a grimace. She was trembling from head to foot.

Olbeck looked at her, his jaw sagging. In a dim and distant part of her mind, she could recognise the hurt that she'd just inflicted beginning to surface on his face, but that was locked away where she couldn't get at it, drenched as she was in shock and furious anger. *Adopt.* Olbeck *knew* how she felt about that, he *knew* what she'd been through, and here he was, all happy and excited; never mind that Kate's heart had just been stamped into a bloody pulp on the floor.

"Kate," Olbeck said quietly. "I know you don't mean that."

"You can't! You can't! If you do that I'll never speak to you again, never, never—" She couldn't say any more; her words were lost in a flood of sobs.

"Kate—" Olbeck tried to speak but she turned and ran from the kitchen. She pulled frantically at the front door. Olbeck called something from the kitchen but she didn't stay to hear what it was; she wrenched the front door open and almost fell over Jeff, who was just outside with a wrapped bottle in his arms. She saw the gold top and knew it was champagne. They actually expected her to *celebrate* with them. By this time, she was crying so hard she could barely see.

"Kate!" Jeff exclaimed in horror. "What's wrong?"

She said nothing but barged her way past him. He gave a shout of surprise and dropped the bottle of champagne. It hit the stone flags of the front porch and exploded in a shower of bubbles and glass, and Kate, by this time at the garden gate, was horribly, viciously glad. She ran down the street towards the main road without a backward glance.

Chapter Thirteen

Trixie Arlen's funeral took place the next day. The weather was suitably funereal; the sky was blanketed with dark grey clouds, and a chill wind whipped the coats and scarves of the mourners as they arrived at the church. The little village of Marshfield, three miles from the farmhouse where Trixie Arlen had died, had never seen so many people. The black limousines of the funeral procession moved slowly through the thronged streets. Cameras and mobile phones were raised high above the heads of the crowds, filming the hearse as it drove by. Paparazzi were clustered around the lychgate to the church, ready to snap anyone who passed through it.

Kate, who'd driven down alone, had to park almost in the next village and walk a mile before she could get close to the church. She was dressed in her black suit and carried another bunch of white roses, just as she had to the funeral of John Miller. What a contrast to this that had been. There must have been three hundred people actually attending the service, not to mention the crowds waiting impatiently outside the church. Kate regarded herself in the rear view mirror for a long moment and then took a pair of dark glasses from her handbag. There was no way she could walk into a church with eyes as red-raw as hers were, even if this was a funeral.

She locked the car and began the long walk to the churchyard, clutching her bouquet. There was an ache in her chest, a physical pain that made her stop once in a while and press her hand against her breastbone. *My heart is actually broken. I've lost my best friend, I've lost Anderton, and I've failed my exams.* Kate stopped for a moment to catch her breath. For a second she felt dizzy and didn't think she could walk another step without falling over. All she wanted to do was go home, hide under the duvet and never leave again; just moulder away beneath the bedclothes until all the pain was gone.

The church was so crowded there was no possibility of getting a seat. Kate propped herself against a chilly stone wall at the back. She was glad that she was wearing a pair of flat shoes, insomuch that she was capable of feeling glad about anything. The coffin was one of those fancy painted jobs, garlanded with roses and strewn with lavender; Kate could smell it even at the back of the church. She found herself wondering what it had cost. All that money for a box that was going to be buried in the ground. Put me in a cardboard box when the time comes, she thought bleakly. Who would come to her funeral? Her brother and sisters, perhaps. They were about the only people in her life she hadn't managed to alienate.

The voice of the vicar droned on. *Eternal life*... the way Kate was feeling, that would be a punishment, not a blessing. She tried to switch her thoughts, tried to find something positive to think about but could think of nothing. To her horror, she felt tears begin to well up again, and she blinked frantically, trying to stop them and realised she couldn't. She felt in her handbag for a tissue. At least at a funeral you didn't need a reason for crying. Restrained sobs and whimpers rose from the packed church. How many of these people had actually known Trixie?

After what felt like several years, the service came to an end. As Kate was near the entrance she was able to leave the church before the masses. She walked over to the churchyard wall, unsure of whether she should wait. She'd caught sight of Olbeck as she arrived and felt a lurch of nausea. The furious anger she'd felt last night had dissipated, just as she needed it. Now all she felt was shame. Olbeck had given her what was probably the happiest news of his life last night and what had she done? Screamed and shouted and abused him. *You're a monster, Kate.* And poor Jeff, as well. They would probably never speak to her again, and who could blame them? All because she had never got over what had happened to her in her teens? Wasn't it time that she did? Wasn't it time she actually grew up and acted like an adult? *You're thirty-one, Kate. Act your bloody age, for once.*

Kate came back to reality with a start. She'd been reprimanding herself in the privacy of her own head for so long that it was quite a shock to realise that most of the mourners had already departed. She could see Jacob Arlen over by the entrance to the church, talking to a tall bald man. Kate looked at the man curiously. He looked vaguely familiar. Was he a celebrity? There had been several at the funeral, gawped at and gossiped about in whispered tones: several television presenters, an actress, a model. Where had she seen him? Kate pondered it a moment longer and then dismissed the bald man from her mind. She had enough to worry about.

She was dreading bumping into Olbeck but he'd clearly already left. He must have seen her standing over by the wall – the way the churchyard was laid out, there was no way of missing her – but he hadn't come over to talk to her. Despite understanding why, Kate felt her heart sink even further. I have to talk to him, I have to apologise, she told herself, and she even got out her phone and brought up his number before putting it away. Not yet. She didn't even know what to say.

Kate looked around for another of her colleagues but couldn't see anyone, not even Theo. She sighed and pushed herself away from the churchyard wall. A long walk back to her car and then a lonely journey back to Abbeyford. Sooner or later, she was going to have to face the reality of work. She was going to face Olbeck – and Anderton. *God.* Kate sighed again and pushed her hands into the pockets of her suit. She began to walk back to her car, head bowed against the spitting rain.

Chapter Fourteen

"WANT TO HEAR SOMETHING INTERESTING?"

"What's that?" Kate had to fight to sound interested. Theo didn't appear to notice her lack of enthusiasm. He was leaning forward over this desk, his dark eyes bright.

"You know that hotel that Arlen was staying in the night of Trixie's death?"

"Do I?"

"You should do. The Granchester. He stays there a lot apparently, the desk clerks all know him."

"Right," said Kate, wondering if there was a point to this.

"*Well*, apparently that night the night porter saw him leave the hotel. About eleven pm."

That got Kate's attention. She sat up a little. "Right," she said again, but more alertly.

Theo's eyes were sparkling. "So, if the night porter's telling the truth – and I can't see why he would lie – then—"

Kate finished the sentence for him. "Then that's Arlen's alibi smashed to pieces."

"Exactly." Theo sat back in his chair and folded his arms. "What if he drove back to his place that night, persuaded his wife to OD – or did it for her – and then pretended to find her first thing in the morning?"

"Yes," said Kate slowly, thinking. "It's possible. But why?"

Theo waved a hand airily. "Oh, motives, motives. I'm not going to worry my head about *why* at the moment. I just want to know if that's how it actually happened."

Kate leapt up. "You're absolutely right, Theo. Let's go, shall we?"

"Hold on a sec. We just need to run it past Mark first."

Kate's stomach clenched. She'd successfully avoided Olbeck all morning, burying her head in paperwork whenever he walked past her desk, refusing to catch his eye when she could feel him staring at her through the glass wall of his office. She wondered whether it was obvious to anyone else that they weren't speaking. During her entire conversation with

Theo, a small part of her had been quite impressed that she'd sounded so normal, considering most of her still felt that death would be quite an attractive alternative to carrying on living.

"You do that," she said hastily. "I'm going to get my coat."

They walked past Anderton's office on the way to the car park but this time, the blinds were closed. Kate wondered whether he was in there with his new woman again. She felt a twist of jealous paranoia and told herself to get a grip. Any more of that and you'll literally go mad, she told herself. Keep a lid on it.

As they waited to join the main road – traffic was always heavy at this point in the morning – Kate let her gaze drift to the newspaper vendor stand on the pavement. The new edition of the Abbeyford Gazette had been published and the large photograph on the front page made Kate gasp.

"Stop! Stop for a minute, Theo?"

"What?" Theo asked, confused.

"Hold on a second." Kate hopped out of the car and ran over to the stand. She bought a paper and brought it back.

"What *are* you doing?" Theo asked.

Kate stabbed a finger at the picture on the front page. "This guy, I knew I knew him. He was at Trixie Arlen's funeral."

Theo looked. "Michael Dekker. Of course you know him. He's about the richest guy in Abbeyford."

Kate was reading the article attached to the photograph. "He's just made a big donation to Outreach. You know, the drug and alcohol charity."

153

She read a few more sentences. "Why would he be at Trixie Arlen's funeral?"

Theo rolled his eyes. "'Cos his son used to go out with her, didn't he? The musician guy. What was his name?"

Kate shrugged. "I don't know. I don't know who you're talking about."

Theo put the car into gear and they finally drove off. "James Gantry!" he shouted triumphantly before they'd gone fifteen yards.

"Oh, *him*," said Kate. "I didn't know that was Michael Dekker's son. Whatever happened to him?"

"He died."

"Seriously? What of?"

"Drugs overdose."

Kate snorted, unsympathetically. "God, how original. Is there a single musician who's managed to off himself or herself in a totally new and thought provoking way?"

Theo didn't dignify that with an answer and Kate, a little ashamed of herself, didn't say anything else for a while.

"Actually," she said after a few minutes of silence. "I might give Michael Dekker a call. It would be useful to talk to someone who knew Trixie Arlen back in the nineties."

"Would it?" asked Theo. Then he cursed and sounded the horn at a black BMW who had cut him up.

"Careful," said Kate. "Yes, I think it would." She hesitated and said "I can't help feeling that Trixie's past is important. I don't know why but...that's what I think."

"Knock yourself out," said Theo.

They finally cleared the clogged streets of Abbeyford and headed towards the motorway. Kate kept checking her phone, thinking she might see a text from Olbeck. Stupid, she told herself, putting it away for the umpteenth time. He's not going to contact me. She closed her eyes briefly, that overwhelming rush of misery engulfing her again. I have to say sorry, she thought. He has to forgive me, because if he doesn't, I don't know what I'm going to do.

For once, Theo wasn't playing hip-hop or garage at ear-bleeding levels on the car stereo. Instead, there was quite a serious talk show playing quietly in the background. Kate listened with half an ear to the presenter and guest talking about the upcoming films due to be released that month. She and Olbeck used to go to the cinema together quite frequently. God, this was ridiculous, everything reminded her of her friend. This is worse than a relationship breaking down, Kate thought.

"You're quiet today," Theo said as they joined the M4, and Kate started guiltily.

"Just got a lot on my mind."

Theo raised an eyebrow. "Who is he?"

Kate half laughed. "There are other things in the world that cause trouble other than sex, Theo. Did you know that?"

"There are?" Theo asked, in mock-shock.

Kate rolled her eyes but she also smiled. After a moment, she pulled her mind back onto the job. "Does Arlen know we're coming?"

"Nope."

"Good," said Kate. "Let's scare him a little."

Theo nodded. "I had the CCTV checked that night at The Granchester. The clerk wasn't lying. Arlen did leave, late. You can clearly see him driving away and he doesn't come back."

"Really? That's excellent, Theo." Kate felt another unpleasant emotion, this time annoyance at herself for not having the idea first. I've to get a grip, she admonished herself privately. My career is all I've got left. Aloud, she asked "It would be worth pulling any CCTV around the Arlen's farmhouse the night of Trixie's death, wouldn't it? If there is any. Rural places often don't have many cameras."

"Yep," said Theo, moving into the fast lane to overtake a truck. "We'll do that when we get back."

"Are we going to tell Arlen that we've got him leaving The Granchester on camera?"

"Let's see," said Theo. "Let's see what he comes up with before we hit him with the evidence."

They made good time until they reached Putney, where they hit the first of the traffic jams extending from Putney Bridge. Forty minutes later, when the car had advanced all of thirty feet, Kate wondered whether she should suggest abandoning the car and taking the underground.

Eventually they made progress again. Kate watched the glittering surface of the Thames as they drove across the bridge. London had never appealed to her as a place of work or as a place to live. Fine for a visit, but it was too big, too busy; the ancient city took no prisoners. She thought with longing for a moment of the old houses of Abbeyford, the rolling green hills that surrounded the town, the familiar faces that she saw every day. No, she wouldn't want to swap that, not for all the culture, clubs, bars and shops in the world.

Arlen's office on Cheapside was indistinguishable from all the other city offices and financial institutions. Huge walls of plate glass, carefully tinted so visibility from the street was minimal, tight security once you were past the glossy girls of the reception desk. An atrium with a jungle of equally glossy plants, and glass lifts scudding up and down to the many different floors.

Kate watched Arlen's face closely as she and Theo approached. He stared at them as if he couldn't believe his eyes, but she couldn't work out if he was apprehensive that they had come to arrest him or just bracing himself for the anguish of more revelations connected to his wife's death.

"Good morning, Mr. Arlen," Theo said, as Kate shut the door of his office behind them.

"Good morning, officers," replied Arlen stonily. "What can I do for you?"

"I can see you're surprised to see us," Kate said, sitting down opposite him. Theo took the other chair.

"I must confess I am."

Kate and Theo exchanged glances. "Perhaps you'd like to confess to something else as well?" suggested Theo. Kate hid a wince. A bit too obvious, too quickly, surely...

Arlen's frown grew deeper. "I afraid I don't know what you're talking about."

Kate jumped in before Theo could say anything else. "In your statement concerning the night on which your wife died, you stated that you'd stayed the night in The Granchester Hotel on Westbury Street, EC1, and left very early the next morning in order to drive home."

"Yes," said Arlen, clearly realising that Kate hadn't yet finished but just as clearly wanting to say something. "That's ri—"

"You don't wish to amend that statement at all?"

"What do you mean?"

"I mean, do you wish to amend your statement at all?"

Arlen risked a strained smile. "No. No I don't believe so."

There was a moment's silence. Kate hung back, happy to let Theo deliver the blow. He didn't disappoint.

"We have a credible eye-witness, and CCTV footage, that shows you leaving The Granchester and driving from their car park at about eleven pm that evening. Not five-thirty am the following morning, as you said in your statement."

Arlen said nothing. His face remained impassive, but the colour slowly mounted until his entire face turned a dull brick red.

"Do you have anything to say, Mr. Arlen?" Kate asked after a moment.

There was another long silence, and then Arlen spoke in a low voice. "I'm not saying anything until I can speak to my lawyer."

Kate and Theo looked at one another again. Kate was heartened to find that they had shared a flash of unspoken understanding, just as she used to have with Olbeck. The following jab of pain caught her unawares and she broke eye contact.

"We'll continue this conversation down at Abbeyford Station then, sir," said Theo, getting up.

Arlen remained seated. "Is that an order, officer?"

Theo smiled a deceptively charming smile. "No, it's a request. If you refuse that request, however, we will arrest you. Understood?"

Kate saw Arlen's throat ripple as he swallowed.

She watched his gaze go to the open plan space beyond his office, the multitude of desks staffed by his underlings and colleagues already casting curious glances over at them. A small sadistic part of her was hoping he would refuse. She would love to slap some cuffs on him and parade him through the goggling crowd of finance workers.

It was not to be, however. Arlen, whatever else he may be, was clearly not stupid. He nodded abruptly and got up without a further word. The three of them walked back across a silent floor but even as the door closed behind them, as they waited for the lift, Kate could hear the whispers begin to start, rising in a slow hissing wave of muted sound.

Chapter Fifteen

Michael Dekker lived in one of the biggest houses that Kate had ever seen. It was beautiful; an isolated Georgian stone mansion surrounded on all four sides by carefully tended and landscaped gardens – grounds, really, *garden* was too reductive a term for something this size. Nestled at the bottom of a hollow, surrounded on all sides by steep green hills and patches of woodland, it didn't seem like a family home at all, but more like something the National Trust might acquire. Kate almost expected to find a ticket booth and a coach car park beyond the high walls that surrounded the house.

Michael Dekker apparently lived in this enormous place alone. Was he married? Kate realised she didn't know anything about him, apart from the fact that he was a philanthropist, whose patronage was particularly aimed at addiction charities, and that he'd had a semi-famous son who'd died young.

A woman answered the door, dressed in a smart

black dress. Clearly the housekeeper, she was small, young, with sallow skin and black hair tied back in a neat ponytail. Smiling and silent, she examined Kate's identification carefully and bobbed her head in acknowledgement before ushering Kate through the house, through a variety of enormous, beautifully furnished and appointed rooms, before showing her into a vast orangery that ran half the length of the house.

Michael Dekker was sitting in a white wickerwork chair, staring out through the windows of the orangery at the marvellous view beyond, a panoramic vista of rolling hills, forests and the glittering silver thread of a distant river running through it. Would you ever get tired of that view? Kate wondered. She doubted it. She decided to make that her first question.

"What's that? Oh, no, not at all. Well, you can't blame me, can you, Detective Sergeant? It's sublime." Dekker indicated another wickerwork chair opposite and Kate seated herself. "Can I offer you a drink?"

"I'd love a cup of tea, thanks."

Dekker nodded and raised his eyebrows at his housekeeper, who stood waiting patiently at the entrance to the orangery. She bobbed her head again in understanding and left.

"Now, what can I do for you, DS Redman?" There was a faint hint of a South African accent in Dekker's voice. He was a big man, barrel-chested and bald-headed, with thrusting shoulders and rather pale blue eyes.

"Well, firstly, thank you for seeing me at such short notice, Mr. Dekker. I appreciate you must be a very busy man."

"Well, that's true. But I hope I can help."

Kate tore her gaze from the view with difficulty and shifted in her chair to face Dekker. "I wanted to talk to someone who knew Trixie Arlen, particularly someone who knew her back in – well, in her heyday; I suppose you could call it that. Back in the nineties."

Dekker rubbed his chin. His pale eyes regarded Kate thoughtfully. "Well, I don't know if I can say I knew Trixie well, DS Redman—"

"Call me Kate."

"Very well. Kate. I have known her – I mean, I knew her for years, but I wouldn't have said I ever knew her *well*."

"Well, anything you might be able to tell me could help."

There was a tinkle of china at the entrance to the orangery. The housekeeper had brought an entire tray of tea things: a silver teapot, delicate china cups and a milk jug, a sugar bowl with silver tongs. There was even a plate of expensive-looking biscuits. Again, Kate had the odd impression that she was in a National Trust tearoom, rather than a family home. Perhaps it wasn't a family home, though. She asked Dekker if he'd lived here long.

"Oh, yes. For over twenty years now. My son grew up here."

Dekker's hand trembled a little as he poured the tea. Kate quickly gave her condolences.

"Thank you," said Dekker, emotions under control again. "It's a long time ago now but it still – catches me, I suppose you could say. A child shouldn't die before his parents."

"No, I agree," said Kate, fervently. "Do you have any other children?"

"No. David was my only son. My wife died a few years ago." Dekker passed Kate her teacup and looked around him at all the luxury and splendour. "This place is too big for me, really. I rattle around in here like a...like a bad penny." He gave a short laugh. "I got to know Trixie through David, you know. They were an item for a short while."

"Yes, so I understand."

"She was a very sweet girl, you know. Very lively and vivacious. She and David were very fond of each other for a while, but it didn't last. Perhaps those kind of relationships never do."

"Those kind of relationships?" queried Kate.

Dekker chuckled. "'Showbiz relationships', I suppose you'd call them. Celebrities. David was becoming quite famous for his music when he and Trixie got together. She was the more famous one though, I suppose. At that time. Everyone knew her at that time."

"Why did they split up?"

Dekker shrugged. "I don't think there was any particular reason. They drifted apart, or realised they weren't right for one another, perhaps. David never told me anything specific."

"So there wasn't any – animosity?" asked Kate. She'd almost finished her tea. It was so good she wondered whether she could ask for another cup.

"More tea?" asked Dekker, clearly reading her mind. "Animosity? Oh no. They remained friendly. They were friends right up until David...until David died." Dekker's eyes filmed over and he blinked rapidly several times. "My wife wanted Trixie to read at his funeral."

"And did she?" Kate held out her cup for a refill.

"No. No, not in the end." Dekker dextrously topped up Kate's cup. "I think we both – we all thought that it wouldn't have been a good idea after all. She was devastated by his death – Trixie was, I mean. She said she wouldn't have been able to do it without having hysterics or something. We didn't want to push her."

Kate sipped her fresh tea appreciatively. "I saw you at Trixie's funeral. Do you know her husband well?"

"No. No, not at all. I think that was the first time I'd ever spoken to him. I hadn't really had any contact with Trixie for years, you know. I went to the funeral more out of respect for her memory than anything else. We'd pretty much lost contact over the years. It was a surprise to me to find out that she lived so close. I only realised she'd moved from London when I saw her out and about in the spring this year."

"Did you renew your friendship?"

Dekker shook his head. "No. I think I had thoughts about looking her up and going to see her again properly, but I think – well, I decided that there wouldn't be much point. We were never real friends, you know. We didn't have much in common. David was the only real link between us."

Kate nodded. "I understand. When you knew Trixie back in the nineties, did you – were you aware that she was ever involved with drugs?" Dekker's face flickered and Kate knew that this would probably be a painful subject for him, given his son's death but she had to ask. "I'm sorry, but it could be important."

"That's fine," said Dekker heavily. "I understand. In answer, I don't know. I don't remember ever seeing her take drugs or even talk about them but then, that doesn't mean that she wasn't involved in some way."

"Did Trixie meet her first husband after her relationship with your son ended?"

Dekker proffered the tea pot again and Kate

shook her head with some regret. "Ivo Wright? Yes, Trixie and David and Ivo all knew each other. David and Ivo being musicians, they moved in the same circles. I'm not sure exactly when Trixie and Ivo became a couple but they didn't get married until after David died, I'm pretty sure of that."

Kate carefully placed her empty cup back on the tea tray. She thought once again of how much tragedy Trixie Arlen had experienced in her relatively short life. Perhaps it wasn't so surprising that she'd turned to heroin again – if indeed she had and hadn't had it forcibly injected. Wasn't morphine supposed to be the most effective pain killer? Perhaps I ought to try it, she thought to herself, trying to make an internal joke but instead feeling bleaker than ever.

"Thanks very much, Mr. Dekker, you've been very helpful," said Kate, as she said her goodbyes. In truth, there wasn't much in what he'd told her but she felt sorry for him. He was clearly dreadfully lonely.

"Please do come back if you need to ask me anything else," said Dekker, confirming Kate's previous thought.

"I will indeed. Thank you."

The neat little housekeeper showed Kate to the door and bobbed her head again in response to Kate's thanks. The door shut behind her softly as Kate was halfway down the flight of steps that led to the gravelled driveway. Before she drove away, Kate stood for a moment, looking up at the beautiful façade of the house. A solitary late flower drooped on the stem of the climbing rose that garlanded the front entrance. There was a flicker of movement in one of the windows on the ground floor but the visibility was too limited for Kate to make out who it was. She got into her car and fumbled for the radio, needing to hear something cheerful. All of a sudden, she felt incredibly sad. *I need Mark, I need him to forgive me.* She turned the key in the ignition, blinking hard, and turned the car in a slow circle, leaving Michael Dekker's beautiful, empty, melancholy house behind.

Chapter Sixteen

SHE WAS ALMOST BACK IN Abbeyford when her phone rang; the thing never rang when there was a convenient place to pull over. Cursing, Kate drove on until she found a lay-by and pulled the car in, grabbing for the phone just as it fell silent.

She recognised the number – it was the main number of the pathology labs. With a stab of guilt, she realised Doctor Telling had been trying to get hold of her for several days. Quickly, she redialled the number and was directed through to the doctor's office.

"I'm so sorry for taking so long to call you back," Kate confessed, once she'd introduced herself. "Unforgivable, Kirsten, sorry."

Doctor Telling sounded, for her, rather terse. Kate couldn't exactly blame her. "Yes, I really did need to speak to you quite urgently, Kate. When you didn't call me I contacted DI Olbeck, because what I had to tell you couldn't really wait."

Shit. That was all Kate needed; Olbeck on her

case professionally as well as socially. "I'm really, really sorry. What was it you wanted to tell me?"

Doctor Telling wasn't being terse, Kate realised; she was worried. A little finger of apprehension poked her in the stomach. "We've been running some further tests on the samples of Trixie Arlen's blood and also the drug that you found in her bedroom," said Doctor Telling.

"Yes?" prompted Kate.

"As you know, the results of the first post mortem were inconclusive," Doctor Telling continued. "We were waiting for the results of the more detailed toxicity tests before we could confirm the definitive cause of death. We've now received those results."

"Yes," said Kate. That sense of unease was growing.

Doctor Telling's soft voice was not made for drama but what she said next made Kate gasp. "It wasn't the heroin that killed her."

"It *wasn't*?"

"No. There were significant quantities of heroin detected in her blood but we found another chemical composition which was almost certainly the cause of death."

"What chemical?" asked Kate, feeling suddenly cold.

Doctor Telling hesitated. "It's unusual. So unusual that I actually had to consult a colleague who's more of a specialist in biochemistry. He believes it's a derivative of a legal anaesthetic called Sulatenil."

"Right," said Kate, none the wiser. "So what exactly are you telling me? Trixie was injecting herself with something other than heroin? Or taking heroin and this other drug as well?"

"No. Not at all. The heroin that Trixie was using has been mixed with this Sulatenil. Sulatenil causes significant respiratory depression and can cause sudden respiratory arrest in high enough doses. The proportion of Sulatenil in this batch of heroin was very high. Trixie would have died almost instantly after injecting herself."

"I see," said Kate. "Is it – it's not normal to have this Sula-whatsit mixed in with a street drug then?"

Doctor Telling hesitated again. "I'm not a drugs expert, Kate. All I can advise is that I've never come across it before."

"Right," said Kate. "We'll have to look into it. I've got a few people I can consult."

"Yes, I think you should. If I might make a suggestion, I think we should also be testing the blood samples from the other overdose victims we've been examining this past month, to see if there's a connection."

"Yes. Yes, please do," said Kate. That finger of unease had become a fist, pressing hard into her stomach. "If there's a batch of contaminated heroin out there, then God knows how many more people might be affected."

"Yes, I know," said Doctor Telling. "Hence the urgency of my call."

Kate winced, but silently. She deserved that. "Thanks so much, Kirsten," she said, humbly. "If I heard right, you've already advised Mark – I mean, DI Olbeck – of this?"

"Yes, just before I spoke to you."

That meant Anderton would know already. Kate didn't need to call him. Her misery over Olbeck had been so acute she'd almost forgotten her meltdown over Anderton and his new woman. The remembrance caused her a little jab of pain, but that was almost immediately swept aside by the rising sense of urgency. What the hell should she do first, given this news? How many other people were out there, preparing their injections, heating the powder over a flame, drawing up the lethal liquid into the syringe? How many more had actually done so and were now lying undiscovered, cold and still? Kate actually shuddered. She thanked Doctor Telling once more, told her to call her the second they had the results from the tests they were going to run on the other victims, and then said goodbye. She thought for a moment, fighting the urge to put her head in her hands. Her heart was actually thudding. She grabbed up her phone and called Stuart, praying that he'd answer the phone.

"Kate! Hello, sweetheart, what gives? Have I forgotten lunch?"

"No, nothing like that. Stuart, you've taken plenty of drug awareness courses, haven't you? I know you did undercover with a few drug rings."

Stuart sounded amused. "Blimey, that's going back a few years. But yeah, I did. What do you want to know?"

"When dealers cut their drugs, what do they normally use?"

The amusement had faded from Stuart's voice. "This sounds serious."

"It could be. Please, Stuart, I need to know. They normally use, I don't know, icing sugar or something? I don't know, tell me!"

"All right, all right, keep your hair on. Now, what's this all about?"

"I can't go into that at the moment." Kate hated reminding Stuart that he was no longer a police officer but sometimes he needed a little refresher. "All right, specifically, would a heroin dealer cut his drugs using a really strong anaesthetic?"

There was a silence on the end of the phone. Then Stuart said, slowly, "Not usually. The dealers need to cut the smack with something that mimics it in looks and effects. Something that would be water-soluble as well. They might use something that would exacerbate the effects if they could get away with it. Then the punters would think they

173

were getting top-quality gear and come back for more, whereas actually the dealers making even more money by watering down the actual heroin. What's the anaesthetic?"

"I can't remember the actual name," Kate lied. "But we think it's a derivative of a legal anaesthetic."

She could hear Stuart breathing on the other end of the line. "That's really strange, actually," he said in a quiet tone. "Anything like that is going to be expensive. Why would you use an expensive substance to cut another expensive substance, when the whole point is to make more profit?"

"That's what I thought," said Kate. She wondered if Stuart could hear the faint tremor in her voice.

Stuart cleared his throat. "There have been a few cases where heroin has been contaminated with anthrax spores. Several people died last year, do you remember?"

Kate didn't but she made an agreeing noise. "Yes, but anthrax – that would be a natural contamination, wouldn't it? I mean, someone hasn't deliberately introduced anthrax to a batch of heroin?"

"Oh, no, not at all. The spores might get in through the supply chain at some point but it would be accidental, not deliberate."

"And the victims wouldn't die – well – instantly, would they?" asked Kate. "They would get sick but it would take some time to actually die of anthrax. Is that right?"

"Oh yeah. It could take weeks."

"So in fact, it's nothing like what we've got here then," said Kate, with an edge to her tone.

"Sorry," said Stuart, sounding a little sheepish. "That was the only quick comparison I could come up with. Yes, you're right, Kate. This is something different."

"So what do you think now?"

Stuart hesitated. "I can't say for certain but it may be that this batch of heroin going round has been deliberately contaminated with a lethal substance."

In the silence that followed, Kate could hear Stuart's breathing again, a little faster this time, echoed by the fast beats of her own heart. "Oh, God," she said in a low voice.

"Yeah."

There was another silence and then Kate roused herself from the depths of her anxiety. "Thanks, Stuart. Thanks for your help. I've got to go."

"No worries. Go and do the right thing."

"I will. And Stuart—"

"Yeah?"

"Don't even think of leaking this to the press. I mean it. If you do, I will literally never speak to you again. Ever."

Stuart snorted. "You need the press to be *on* this! You need to get the word out. Otherwise you're going to be knee-deep in dead junkies before the week's out—"

"I *mean* it. We need to work out a media campaign, you *know* that."

Stuart relented. "Yeah, I know. Don't worry. You've got my word."

"Thanks. You're a star," said Kate. "I need to go now but seriously – thanks."

"You're welcome. Keep me posted, yeah?"

"Will do."

After she'd said goodbye, Kate brought Olbeck's number up in her phone. Her thumb hovered above the button, on the verge of pressing it. Then she shook her head and put it away in her bag, clipping her seatbelt back on and flooring the accelerator, leaving the layby with a thin wail of skidding tires.

Chapter Eighteen

As Kate arrived back in the office, she virtually ran into Olbeck as he was walking out into the corridor. They both collided with an 'oof' of surprise and each staggered back a few feet.

"Sorry," gasped Kate automatically. Then reality kicked in. It was the first time she'd spoken to Olbeck since she'd screamed obscenities at him in his kitchen.

He didn't look as though he'd forgotten that. "Kate, I was looking for you."

"You were?" asked Kate, trying to sound unconcerned. The anxiety about the potentially lethal batch of heroin somewhere out in Abbeyford was immediately replaced by the crippling sense of shame she'd carried around with her since she and Olbeck had fallen out.

"Yes," said Olbeck, face impassive. "I've just had a call. I need you to come with me."

Professional curiosity peeked its way above

Kate's emotional state. "Don't tell me it's another overdose?" she asked, quickly.

Olbeck looked surprised, and then his face cleared. "Oh, you've spoken to Doctor Telling then? We can talk about that on the way. No, this might be different. I won't know until we've had a look."

"Right—"

"Let's go, then." For a moment, superficially, everything seemed to have gone back to normal. The next second, Kate realised with a sinking feeling that the anger and hurt seemed to still be very much there.

"I must just get my stuff. I'll meet you at the car."

She ran into the office, flipped a hand at Theo and grabbed up her bag. She was still wearing her coat and was aware of the sweat inching down her back beneath the heavy material. It didn't help her feel much calmer.

Driving away from the station, the air inside the car thickened with unspoken thoughts. Kate stared blankly through the windscreen, feeling utterly miserable. This was her best friend, her closest colleague, and the two of them were like strangers. Worse than strangers, they were like enemies. Tears rose in her eyes and before she knew what she was doing, she had turned to Olbeck.

"I'm so, so, sorry. Mark, I'm so sorry. I could cut out my tongue. I'd give anything to take it back, anything—"

To her shame, her voice had thickened so much she couldn't go on. Kate dropped her head, realised that was a mistake when the tears began to drop onto her jeans, and raised it again. She was aware that the tight knot that she'd felt in her chest ever since that awful night had loosened as she uttered the first apology. She made a mammoth effort at control and said it again. "I'm really, really sorry. I don't know how I can make it up to you."

"All right, all right," Olbeck said, and Kate could see the tightness around his jaw loosening a little. He flicked on the indicator and brought the car into the side of the road before pressing the hazard light button on. Then he turned undid his seatbelt and turned to face Kate.

"I'm sorry," she said again. She wanted to say something else but those two words seemed to be the only ones her mouth was capable of forming.

"You really hurt me," Olbeck said softly. They were staring at one another like lovers. Kate could only shake her head and he must have seen the misery in her face because in the next moment, they'd flung themselves at one another and were hugging each other tight.

Kate cried properly then, soaking Olbeck's shoulder. She could feel his unsteady breathing as she held him and knew he was pretty close to tears himself.

They only hugged for a few moments. Then in

mutual agreement, they sat back and looked at one another. The tension had eased a little. Kate took Olbeck's hands.

"I don't have any real excuse," she said in a low voice. "All I can say is that you caught me on probably the worst day of my life. No, that's not true. The worst day was when I – you know – when I gave him away."

"I know," said Olbeck. "And *I'm* sorry. If I'd had a bit more tact, I would have realised that you would have found that really hard to hear."

Kate was shaking her head. "No, no, Mark. It's my fault. I have to – I have to get over that. I think you and Jeff will be brilliant parents. *Brilliant.* I just hate myself for what I said. I was just lashing out and it was unforgivable, I'm sorry." Her voice wobbled again and she carried on quickly, before it could break. "I have to apologise to Jeff as well. I'm going to do that straight after work tonight if he'll be in."

"He's okay," said Olbeck. "We were worried about you. It's not like you to be so – so volatile. Not even around that subject."

Kate hung her head. "I know. I don't know why – yes, I do know why. But we'll have to talk about that some other time. All I can say is that I am really, truly happy for you and Jeff getting married and adopting, and I'll spend the rest of my life regretting what I said at first." She looked Olbeck straight in the eye, hoping against hope that he believed her. "Because I didn't mean it."

He said nothing but pulled her back into a brief hug again before releasing her. "Come on, we need to get to the scene."

Kate, unable to stop herself, asked in a small voice. "Do you...can you forgive me?"

Olbeck almost smiled. "You've not murdered anyone, Kate. Of course I forgive you." There was a beat of silence and then he added "You're not invited to the wedding, though."

Kate half-gasped, feeling as though she'd just been kicked in the stomach. Olbeck looked stonily ahead for a moment and then his face broke up. He was actually laughing. "I'm joking, you silly cow. Of course you're invited."

For a moment, Kate thought she was going to burst into tears again. Quickly she rubbed her face, pinching the bridge of her nose hard for a second. "Thank you," she said, her voice almost steady.

Olbeck indicated and steered the car back onto the road again. Kate sat back against her seat, heaving a sigh that seemed to come from the depths of her stomach. She had that empty, hollow feeling that came after a really good cry, which was somehow soothing and relieving at the same time. She and Olbeck were friends again. She didn't kid herself that everything was back to normal again – perhaps it would never be – but they were back on the right track. At that moment, Kate didn't care about dirty heroin, or Anderton's sex life, or her failed exams, or anything else. She had her friend back. That, at that moment, was all that mattered.

"Where are we going?" she asked after five minutes had passed. She realised, after the drama of the last few minutes had calmed, that she had absolutely no idea of where they were heading or what they were going to see.

"A body's been found," Olbeck said. She could hear the relief in his voice and knew that he'd been suffering, probably almost as much as she had. She closed her eyes for a moment, swamped with thankfulness that they'd managed to sort it out. Olbeck went on. "At a house in Mellow Abbot. A neighbour noticed the front door was ajar and went in and found it. According to Dispatch, it's a middle-aged man and it's definitely a suspicious death."

"Okay," said Kate. "There's clearly more. What is it?"

Olbeck glanced at her. "Apparently, he's been tied-up, gagged and killed."

Kate blinked. The robbery report from Jack Harker materialised in front of her eyes. Was this the same thing? "Blimey," she said. "Any ideas as yet?"

"Haven't you been collating a few reports on some similar robberies, recently?"

"Yes. Well, I've been meaning to." Kate found herself wondering what she *had* actually achieved over the last month. She put her hands up to her eyes and rubbed them. I need a holiday, she thought. Perhaps I might try Barbados. It had seemed to work for Olbeck.

The car was slowing. Olbeck had spotted the crime tape that had already been stretched across the driveway of a house up ahead. It was a nondescript semi-detached house, built around the 1930s, with a concreted driveway and pebbledash on the exterior walls.

"Do we know who the victim is yet?" asked Kate, as Olbeck drew the car into the kerb.

"He's not been formally IDed yet but the person who found him told us who he was. Adrian Fellowes, aged forty-eight, lecturer in IT at Abbeyford City College."

"That's the vic?" asked Kate, confused.

"Yes. Sorry, yes. His neighbour was the one who found him, she's still there now. Apparently she noticed the front door was wide open and went on in and found him. Margery Wencleve."

By this time, they had passed through the front door and picked their way through the narrow hallway. Uniforms and white-coated SOCOs milled about. The house was cold, whatever residual heat it had contained leaking out of the front door as it was opened and closed by various officers. It was as nondescript on the inside as it had been on the outside. Cheap grey carpet covered the hallway floor and extended into the living room, which ran down the side of the house. Kate followed Olbeck through the doorway to where the body of the unfortunate Adrian Fellowes could be found.

He was fat, naked and slumped on a cheap and nasty looking sofa piece covered in grubby cream fabric. Kate and Olbeck stood silently, taking in the scene. A man bent over the body and as he straightened up and turned to face the two officers, Kate realised it was Andrew Stanton. Such was her ebullience at having made it up with Olbeck, not even this fact could dampen her spirits. She gave him a big smile and he looked at first shocked and then confused.

"Good morning," said Olbeck. "Anything for us yet?"

Apart from that first glance at Kate, Stanton steadfastly refused to look at her. Kate, still in that strange, reckless mood, had to restrain herself from bounding up to him, pinching his cheeks and telling him to get over it. She bit back an extremely inappropriate giggle.

"There's no obvious cause of death," Stanton was saying. "No stab wounds, no ligature marks, no head trauma."

"Really?" Olbeck asked, surprised.

"Yes, you'll have to wait for the post mortem on

this one. I simply can't give you any indication as yet."

Just like Trixie Arlen. "Any sign of drug use? Needle marks, injections, anything like that?" Kate asked.

"No, nothing to indicate intravenous drug use," Andrew said, a little stiffly. "You can see for yourself that he's been indulging in cocaine or amphetamines though. We'll have to run tests to be sure but..."

He indicated the dining table that stood at the back of the room with his head. The top was littered with empty bottles of wine, several glasses with the sticky residue of alcohol in the bottom of them, and what looked like a small bathroom mirror, its surface lightly dusted with white powder.

Kate, having noted this, turned her gaze back to the body. Fellowes' wrists were tied together with what looked like a pair of tights or stockings, his ankles similarly secured. A third stocking gagged his mouth. Kate felt a wrench of pity for him. It was bad enough to die, but to be left in such humiliating circumstances... She wondered whether he had a family and looked around the living room for any photographs, any indication that other people lived here. There was nothing; just an enormous flat-screen television, a pile of computer magazines in the corner of the room, a dusty cactus plant in a chipped blue pot on the windowsill. The room was functional but nothing more, there was no care or attention to comfort, beauty or sophistication.

Olbeck was saying something to her and Kate turned back to him. "What's that?"

"Have a look at him again," Olbeck said. "What's wrong with this picture?"

Kate gave him an old-fashioned look and looked again at the body. "What do you mean?"

"We're assuming this is a potential robbery, right?"

"Yes. Given its similarity to the other cases."

"So, clearly, whoever did this didn't tie him up to make sure he didn't escape. He's not tied to anything, is he? Just – just himself."

Kate nodded. "Yes. But that would fit in with what the previous victim – Jack Harker said. He said he woke up after passing out, or being drugged, tied up."

"Exactly," said Olbeck. "It looks like there's a team or a couple of people out there honey-trapping men into being tied up and then robbed."

"Okay," said Kate. "It's a possibility. But then why kill your victim?"

"Maybe he recognised one of them. Maybe they're getting more aggressive as they go on. Maybe they didn't mean to kill him."

"You don't think that this might be another overdose?" asked Kate in a low voice.

Olbeck looked uneasy. "We won't know until we

have the PM results. But it doesn't look like it, does it?"

"No," Kate admitted. Andrew had stated that he couldn't see any injection marks and given that there was clear evidence of cocaine (or similar) use at the scene, it was different to what had happened at Trixie Arlen's farmhouse. All the same... Kate stood and watched the SOCOs at their work, thinking and frowning. There had never been such a spate of potentially suspicious deaths in Abbeyford, not since she'd arrived here. Could there really be no connection between the cases?

She drifted into the hallway again and wandered into the kitchen at the end of the hallway. It was a small, dank room, just as cheerless and as lacking in personality as the rest of the house. Empty pizza boxes and takeaway food containers were stacked messily by the overflowing kitchen bin. The stove top was clean, if dusty – clearly Mr. Fellows was not much of a cook. A small fridge hummed busily to itself by the back door and a narrow gate-leg table was crammed up against its side, its surface littered with flyers, old newspapers and junk mail. Kate stood in the doorway, wondering whether there was any point to what she was doing. She turned and was about to leave when she felt a sudden pull, a little snag of her consciousness, a jab of something significant. Kate turned slowly and regarded the dirty little kitchen again. What had it been? She swept her gaze slowly over the squalor, wondering what it was that she'd subconsciously noticed. Then she saw it, tucked between a packet of sugar and an empty glass jar on the kitchen counter. A small business card, pink with a flowery black logo. *Home Angels, Domestic Cleaning.*

Kate picked it up with gloved fingers and took it back through to Olbeck.

"Look at this."

He glanced at it and then back at Kate, enquiringly.

"It's probably nothing," said Kate "But Jacob Arlen gave me a card for this company when I asked him where I could find his cleaner. She's someone we still need a statement from."

"Right," said Olbeck, not sounding very convinced. "It probably is nothing, like you say."

"I know, but I'd like to look into it, just in case. If the Arlens and Julian Fellowes shared a cleaner, then that's a link between the two cases."

"Fine with me." Olbeck's attention was clearly elsewhere. "I'm trying to find out what's missing. This looks like a guy who was interested in gadgets, right? I can't see anything around here that looks expensive, except for the TV. Let me talk to that neighbour..."

Muttering to himself, he left the room. Kate could have told him he was too late – several minutes ago she'd looked out the window and seen a white-faced middle-aged woman being shepherded into a patrol car - but she let him go. Kate's eyes went to the dining room table. Several empty glasses there... she looked back at the pathetic chubby corpse of Adrian Fellows and thought back to the first person she'd seen at the station wanting to report a robbery, that sad little man who'd changed his mind and scurried off. Who was out there, targeting lonely single men? Was there really any connection to the overdose deaths that had been occurring, or was that just something that Kate's mind was insisting was the case? Kate rubbed her eyes. After the emotional turmoil of the last few days, it was difficult to stay focused on work. She was exhausted. I really do need a holiday, she thought, and vowed that on the completion or winding down of these cases, she would book one immediately. Somewhere hot and sunny and vacuous, where Kate would have to do nothing more taxing than lie on a sun lounger and drink mocktails.

Cheered by the thought, she went to find Olbeck. He was in the one of the bedrooms upstairs, conferring with one of the uniformed officers, who turned out to be Sergeant Bill Osbourne. Bill raised a large, hairy hand in greeting when he saw Kate approaching.

"Bill's just been telling me that everything valuable is gone," Olbeck said as Kate joined them.

"Everything valuable that you could carry away by hand."

"So you think they came on foot?" asked Kate.

Olbeck nodded. "Would fit in with our theory that whoever these people are, they're meeting up with their victims for an ostensibly social purpose."

Kate raised her eyebrows. "Like a date?"

"Mmm. Might be a 'chance' meeting though, if they're targeting men they think would be likely to invite them home." Olbeck made speech marks in the air with his forefingers.

Kate tried to force her tired brain to think. "I suppose we should see if this Fellowes was on any dating sites, then. Might be a lead there."

"You'll have a job, lass," rumbled Bill Osbourne. "They've taken his laptop, iPad and tablet."

"I'll put the analysts onto it," said Kate, undaunted. "They might be able to find something."

"Okay, good start," said Olbeck. "We'll have the PM results in the next few days which should give us more to go on."

Kate remembered something. She caught Bill Osbourne's arm. "Bill, have the pathology labs been in touch with you about your case – those two dead drug addicts – Pete and Wayne Thingy?"

Osbourne frowned. "Not that I'm aware. Why?"

Quickly Kate explained, with Olbeck chipping in. Bill Osbourne's phlegmatic face was incapable of showing extreme emotion but he did look unsettled.

"Now, there's a thing," he said, once they'd finished. "Contaminated heroin, eh? Nasty."

Kate warned him not to mention it to anyone else. "There'll be a press conference about it any time now, once the info's been primed for the media. But I—" she glanced at Olbeck, "I mean, *we* wondered whether you'd had any more overdoses since we've seen you last?"

Osbourne frowned again, thinking. "Aye. Aye, we have had one, actually. Totally non-suspicious, another known addict. Last week."

Kate opened her mouth to ask and then shut it again, looking again at Olbeck. He was her superior, after all.

He caught the glance and acknowledged it with a tilt of his head. "Could you send me the PM report and anything else you've got on it, Bill? We'll get the labs to run those specific tests to see if it's connected. It'll all help with making a case against whoever is distributing this batch."

"Aye, I'll do that. No problem."

They conferred for a few more minutes before Kate and Olbeck took their leave. They did a last sweep of the house, sidestepping the white-coated SOCOs and technicians and took a last look at the body; a stretcher and body bag had been laid on the floor in front of the sofa, ready to receive its sad cargo. Kate and Olbeck said goodbye to Doctor Stanton, who was too absorbed in his work to reach his usual level of sniffiness with Kate. He actually sounded rather absentmindedly amiable, which made Kate feel quite cheerful as they left the house, despite the surroundings and the exhaustion which was dragging at her.

She leant her head against the back of the car seat as they drove away and fought not to close her eyes. It reminded her of Theo, as they'd driven back from interviewing all of Trixie Arlen's friends, and that in turn reminded her of confronting Jacob Arlen at his office. She struggled back up to a sitting position. "What happened with Arlen? Did he recant his previous statement?"

Olbeck gave a short laugh. "Not that I heard. His lawyer advised him to say no comment to everything and that's exactly what he did."

"Did you do the interview?"

"No. Anderton and Theo took it."

"Really?" Kate bit back the sharp retort she wanted to make, struggled a little and then temptation overcame her. "What, Anderton actually did some work? You *do* surprise me."

Olbeck glanced at her, surprised. "What is it with you at the moment? You're falling out with everybody."

Kate opened her mouth and then shut it again. "Oh, nothing," she said lamely, after a moment. She wanted to tell Olbeck why, in Anderton's case, she had a personal vendetta against him but decided not to. There was time enough to come clean in the future – she didn't want to rock the fragile equilibrium of the friendship she and Mark had managed to salvage after their row.

"So, we've arrested Arlen, then?" she asked, after a short period of silence.

Olbeck raised one shoulder in a kind of shrug. "I'm not sure. That was under discussion when I got the call about this case."

"Okay. Well we'll know soon enough, I suppose," said Kate, and this time she put her head back against the headrest again and closed her eyes. She was asleep in moments.

Chapter Nineteen

THE NEXT DAY SAW KATE, refreshed after the best
night's sleep she'd had in weeks, jumping in the
shower at the sprightly hour of six-thirty am without
even a muttered protest. She let the hot water ease
the night stiffness from her shoulders and thought
about her day ahead.

Priority one was to try and track down the
mysterious cleaner or cleaning company that was
the only known link between the Arlen and the
Fellowes crime scenes. Kate twisted the shower
control to 'off' and stepped out, reaching for her
towel. For a moment, she was assailed by doubt.
Was it a lead worth pursuing? Really? There were
a hundred other things she could be doing. Should
she drop into the office and see if she could sit in
when Arlen was interviewed that morning? Jacob
Arlen had been formally arrested the day before
and the team were going all out to try and get to the
bottom of where he had actually been on the night
of Trixie Arlen's death. They'd pulled his mobile

phone records and the Arlens' bank statements, to see if there was suspicious movement on either of them, but nothing had come up as yet. Perhaps I should try and sit in on that, Kate thought, fingers slipping as she buttoned her shirt in haste. But then, Anderton and Theo had that covered, and she wasn't sure how happy they would be with her if she tried to muscle in at this late stage.

She needed to check with Doctor Telling to see if any other overdose deaths had been attributable to the heroin contaminated with Sulatenil. She needed to check with the analysts to see if there had been a noticeable spike in deaths due to drug use over the past month. When was Anderton planning to do the press conference? Today? Kate pulled on her trousers and zipped them up. God, this was overwhelming, too much to do and not enough time or head space to do it. Think of the holiday, she told herself fervently as she pulled on her shoes and coat. Think of the holiday.

Before she left the house, she tried calling the Home Angels number, to see if she could make herself an appointment with the manager of the firm, but the number just rang and rang until Kate finally hung up. She Googled the name of the firm on her phone but nothing came up in the search results except for the same phone number she'd just tried to call. There was an address on the card that looked to be a unit on one of the industrial sites on the south side of Abbeyford. Kate locked up the house and got into her car, pondering. After a moment's consideration, she keyed the postcode of the business address into her sat nav and turned on the engine.

The satellite guidance system took her to a small industrial estate on the outskirts of Arbuthon Green. Kate drove slowly along the narrow road that led to the address on the business card, which turned out to be a small modern building of maroon brick and white plastic cladding. There were no cars parked on the small forecourt at the front and no lights could be seen behind the plastic blinds at the window. Kate parked the car and got out. There was no answer to her knocks at the door. She tried the handle, just on the off chance, but it was locked. She knocked again, just for luck, but still no one answered. She tried calling the number again and she could faintly hear the telephone ringing inside the office but no one picked up her call.

Well, that was a wasted journey. Kate drove back to the station, trying the number once more just after she locked up her car. No answer. Kate mentally shrugged and made her way to the office.

"Morning," she said to Theo, who was looking through what looked like CCTV pictures. He gave her a vague wave in response. "Is Anderton still interviewing Jacob Arlen?"

Theo finally looked up. He looked tired, his

handsome brown eyes ringed with shadow. "Yeah, he's still at it. We've only got to the end of the day."

Kate nodded in acknowledgement. Once she'd ascertained the interview room number, she made her way there, peeking through the peephole. She could just see the edge of Anderton's shoulder and beyond him, across the table, Jacob Arlen, who looked exhausted. Kate felt a pang of pity for him, which she quickly suppressed. She hesitated, knowing that this might not be a good time to interrupt the interview, but when might she get the chance again? She bit her lip and knocked.

All three men looked surprised to see her. "Sir," she said, for the benefit of Arlen, "Could I have a quick word?"

She meant it for Olbeck but Anderton himself got up and accompanied her outside.

"What's up?" he asked, adding, "Haven't seen you in ages."

He was standing closer to her than he had been for weeks and Kate was disconcerted at the sheer physical response she felt at his nearness. Goddammit, why did she have to find him so attractive? When was she going to get over him?

Trying to keep her mind on the job, she explained as quickly as she could. Anderton raised his eyebrows but made no comment. Instead, he opened the door to the interview room and ushered her inside.

She seated herself next to Olbeck, who obligingly budged his chair over for her. Jacob Arlen looked at her with a frown.

"I've got a very quick question for you, Mr. Arlen," Kate said.

Arlen sighed a long suffering sigh. "No comment."

Kate persisted. "I'm trying to track down someone who might be very important to this case. Could you tell me all you know about your cleaner, Rosa?"

Clearly, whatever Arlen had been expecting Kate to ask, it hadn't been this. "Rosa?" he asked, cautiously. "What do you mean?"

"I'm trying to find her," explained Kate. "But I'm having a lot of trouble. There's no answer at the agency number and I've got no other way of contacting her."

Arlen glanced at his solicitor, an urbane, white-haired man rather like him in looks. The solicitor nodded slightly.

Arlen turned back to Kate. "Well, I can't help you, I'm afraid. I've got no other contact number for her. Trixie dealt with all of that kind of thing."

"But you have seen her?" asked Kate. "Rosa? You could describe her?"

Arlen looked confused. "Yes, I did meet her, a couple of times, at the house. But I don't *know* her..."

"That's fine," said Kate. "Could you just tell me what she looks like?"

Arlen almost shrugged. "I can't remember exactly – she was dark, long dark hair. Very thin. Young, probably not more than twenty-five."

Kate nodded encouragingly but clearly Arlen had reached the limit of his descriptive powers. "I'm afraid that's all I can remember," he finished.

"Is she English?" Kate asked.

Arlen looked confused. "English? No – no, I don't think she is. Polish or Czech, or something like that. She had quite a strong accent."

Kate nodded. "There's nothing else you can tell me about her? You don't know where she lived or anything like that?"

"No," Arlen said. "I don't know anything more about her. She just cleaned our house." This time he looked at Olbeck and Anderton, as if seeking an explanation for Kate's sudden appearance. They stared back at him, impassive, and Kate felt a rush of gratitude to both of them.

"You don't know if she was married?" she persisted.

"I'm sorry, I don't know," Arlen said with distaste. "I really didn't know her at all well. I don't believe I ever spoke to her."

Clearly that was all he was going to give her. Kate believed him when he said he didn't know anything more. Obviously, to a man like him, a cleaner was so lowly as to be almost beneath his notice. Kate was just grateful that he'd even noticed Rosa at all. She thanked him, nodded to Olbeck and Anderton, and left the room, feeling Arlen staring after her as she closed the door behind her.

She made her way back up to the reception area of the station, walking quite slowly as she thought about his response. As it was, she was almost bowled over as a woman came rushing into the station, in a flurry of windswept hair and a cloud of perfume.

It was Kyla Mellors. She gazed around her in what looked like panic, saw Kate and rushed over to her. "Is Jacob here? I heard you'd arrested him – where is he?"

"Calm down, Mrs. Mellors," Kate said, bringing a soothing tone to the fore. She took Kyla by one slender arm and steered her towards some chairs over by the far wall. "How can I help?"

Kyla looked near tears. "I heard you arrested Jacob. Is it true? It can't be true!"

Kate hesitated before answering. "Yes, Mr. Arlen is currently helping us with our enquiries."

The tears spilled over and ran down Kyla's cheeks. "Is it to do with Trixie's death?" she gasped. "Are you thinking that he had something to do with that?"

"I can't comment on that, Mrs.—"

"Because he didn't," said Kyla, vehemently. "He absolutely couldn't have. It's impossible."

Kate leaned forward a little. "Do you want to amend your statement, Mrs. Mellors?"

Kyla bit her lip and brushed the tears from her face. She glanced around the station and then spoke in a low tone. "Is there somewhere we can talk privately?"

Kate took her to one of the nicer interview rooms and gestured to the one fairly comfortable chair. Kyla seated herself. She had the air of a woman bracing herself for a necessary but unpleasant ordeal. Kate propped herself against the desk and raised her eyebrows in an encouraging way, although she was beginning to have an inkling of what it was that Kyla was about to tell her.

Kyla took a deep breath. "Jacob wasn't anywhere near Trixie the night she died because – because he was with me."

Although Kate half-admired her for coming clean, she wouldn't be human without the opportunity to have one little, very little dig. "By 'with you' I assume you mean..."

Kyla was sitting very upright. A tumble of words practically fell from her mouth. "Yes, with me as in we're having an affair. He stayed the night with me and left very early in the morning." As soon as she'd finished her sentence, she fell back into her seat, as if all the strength had left her muscles. After a moment, she said in a shaky voice, "My God, it's such a relief to finally come clean. I didn't think it would be such a relief." She sat forward then and put her face in her hands.

Kate cleared her throat. "How long have you and Mr. Arlen been sexually involved?"

Kyla sat up again. She looked tearful but in control of herself. "About eighteen months. It was wrong, I know it was wrong but..."

"Does your husband know?" Kate asked after Kyla's voice faded away at the end of her sentence.

Kyla shook her head. "No. No, he doesn't. I'm going to tell him though. Today, I'm going to tell him today. I'm going to leave him. I can't be such – such a coward any longer."

Despite herself, Kate pitied her. "Did Trixie know?"

Again, Kyla shook her head. "I don't think so. I don't think Jacob would have told her." She hesitated and then said in a subdued voice, "They didn't really communicate much. He said that she...with Trixie, it was all surface and nothing underneath." Her eyes met Kate's and she flushed. "All right, I know that's the biggest cliché in the world – 'my wife doesn't understand me'. All I can say is that I believed him. I believed Jacob. I *do* believe him."

Kate nodded. "Is there anything else you can tell me, Mrs. Mellors?"

Kyla looked confused. "About – about the affair?"

"Well..." Kate wasn't exactly sure what she was asking herself. She hesitated and then asked, "What was Trixie like? *Really* like?"

She was hoping that Kyla Mellor's newfound

candour would give her some information that perhaps she hadn't had before. But Kyla simply shrugged and said, "I don't know."

"What do you mean? You were friends, weren't you?"

"We thought we were friends. Well, I guess Trixie thought we were friends." Kyla looked down at her hands, at the no-doubt wildly expensive engagement and wedding ring on her left hand. "I wasn't much of a friend to her, was I?" Before Kate could say anything, she looked up at her. "I mean, I really didn't *know* her. It was like Jacob said, all surface. She was nice and friendly and easy to like, but I didn't ever *know* her. She never, ever let me in. Perhaps that's what made it easy, *easier*, to – to do what I did."

Kate shifted a little on the hard edge of the table. "Did you ever take drugs with Trixie?"

Kyla looked shocked. "No. I told you. Never. I wouldn't do that."

"Did you know that Trixie took drugs?"

Kyla's gaze dropped again. "I only know what Jacob told me. He told me about six months ago, that he'd caught her using heroin. Just the once. She swore it was a one-off, apparently."

"Do you think he believed that?"

"I don't think so. We talked about it a couple of times. He said at one point he was thinking about putting a camera in the house, to keep an eye on what she did. I was a bit shocked and I think that put him off the idea. I don't think he ever did it."

Something else that Anderton and Theo could ask their suspect. Except, he wasn't a suspect anymore, was he? Kate found that she believed every word Kyla was telling her. Adulterer he might be, but it looked like Jacob Arlen was nothing more than that.

"Thanks for telling me this, Mrs. Mellors," said Kate. Kyla nodded. She looked worn out but heartily relieved still. "It's a shame you couldn't have been more honest with us at the start of this investigation. You do realise you could be charged with perverting the course of justice?"

Kyla blanched. "Oh my God."

"Yes," said Kate relentlessly. "We don't do this job for fun, you know. Do you know how much time we've wasted already because we weren't given the true facts?"

"I'm so sorry – I just – oh, my God—" Kyla stuttered. Kate continued to frown at her for a moment before she relented.

"The first thing you'll have to do is amend your statement. After that – well, I'll see if I can persuade DCI Anderton not to take things any further."

Kyla nodded and went on nodding jerkily. "Yes of course. Of course I will. I'm sorry."

"Fine. Come with me, then and we'll sort that out now."

Kate got up and Kyla did likewise. At the door, she caught hold of Kate's arm. "I know this is asking a lot, especially after – after what you've just said, but is there – is there any way we can keep this from the press?" she asked, a little desperately.

Kate raised one shoulder in a half-shrug. "I'd like to say yes, Mrs. Mellors, but I'm afraid I can't. These things do have a habit of coming out."

Kyla nodded miserably. Kate was preparing to hand her over to the desk staff when something occurred to her. She took Kyla to one side. "Can I just ask you, did you ever meet Trixie's cleaner, Rosa?"

Kyla blinked but, unlike Arlen, didn't seem to question the relevance of the enquiry. "Rosa? Yes, quite a few times. She was there quite often."

"What was she like? Did you ever talk to her?"

"No. No, I didn't know her to speak to." Kyla was looking a little nervous now. "Is she okay?"

"Rosa? As far as I'm aware. I'm just trying to track her down," said Kate. "Can you tell me what she looked like?"

Kyla hesitated. "Well, she was a bit strange, actually. Really thin. I once thought she might have been quite pretty, if she'd only put on a stone or something. She had long dark hair...I'm not sure what else I can tell you." She paused and then said reluctantly, "There was one thing - she – she had strange eyes. Her pupils were weird, really tiny pupils. Gosh, that sounds really bitchy, doesn't it? I don't mean it like that—"

She was obviously feeling guilty. Kate soothed her and thanked her. Once she'd handed Kyla over to the colleague who would supervise her statement, Kate walked back to her desk, thinking. The description of Rosa, unappealing as it had been, had sparked a memory; some sort of recollection of where she'd heard that description before. The tiny pupils in particular. Kate pondered and then realised with a start that she needed to let Anderton know about Kyla Mellor's confession as soon as she could. She hurried down the steps, abandoning her thoughts about Rosa for the time being.

Chapter Twenty

KATE AND OLBECK ATTENDED ADRIAN Fellowes'
post mortem the next day, and Kate was pleased
to find that Andrew Stanton, who was performing
the operation, had seemingly retained his newfound amiability. He greeted her and Olbeck with
every sign of politeness and that awful stiffness
that used to accompany his every remark to her
had disappeared. In return, she found herself
responding in a more natural, friendly way. It was
one of the most pleasant post mortems she'd ever
experienced.

"Well," Stanton said, once he'd opened up the
chest cavity of the unfortunate Mr Fellowes. "Cause
of death is plain. Myocardial infarction."

"Come again?" said Olbeck.

Stanton grinned. "Common or garden heart
attack. Look here - you can see the severe build-up
of plaque in the coronary arteries. A sudden increase
in physical activity, not to mention ingestion of
cocaine...either of those coupled with a tear in the

plaque would have caused a blood clot that would have interrupted blood flow to the heart. Very common."

Kate and Olbeck exchanged glances. "So it's a natural death, then?" Olbeck asked, to be absolutely clear.

Stanton nodded. "Absolutely."

Olbeck blew out his cheeks. "Is it just me, Kate, or do you suddenly find yourself longing for a straightforward, juicy murder?"

Kate couldn't help smiling. "It is a bit topsy-turvy, isn't it? The death we thought was suspicious turns out not to be, whilst all the so-called normal deaths turn out to be anything but."

"Exactly."

"Mind you," Olbeck went on to say to Kate, as they made their way back to the car after the PM. "It's not *exactly* non-suspicious, is it? Okay, so the poor bloke had a heart attack, but the fact remains that someone tied him up and left him there. Do you think they realised he was dead?"

Kate shrugged. "We won't know unless we find them. Have we got any forensics back yet? Fingerprints or anything?"

"Don't know. I don't think so. We'll start leaning on the labs once we get back."

Olbeck was driving again. Kate tapped her fingers on her legs as they drove along, impatient to actually do something. "Can you do me a favour?"

she asked, as she saw the sign for Arbuthon Green at the junction they were approaching. "Can we just try the Home Angels office again while we're in the area?"

Olbeck looked surprised but nodded. "Okay. It'll only take a minute."

The industrial estate looked just as deserted as it had the first time, with one exception. There was a large black Range Rover parked outside the Office Angels building. Olbeck took one look at it and drove past.

"What—" Kate began but he gestured at her to pipe down. He drove to the end of the street and pulled into the car park of another building, slowing the car and swinging it around to face the way they came.

"What is it?" whispered Kate, tense in her seat.

Olbeck leant forward, staring at the Range Rover. "I know that car," he said quietly. Then he leant forward even more. "Get down," he said suddenly.

Kate didn't stop to ask why. She dived floorwards, as did Olbeck. They exchanged glances from their crouched position on the car seats. Distantly, Kate heard the engine of the Range Rover start up and then the sound of the engine gradually faded away.

Olbeck cautiously eased himself up in his seat and peered through the windscreen again. "It's okay," he said to Kate and she straightened up. "I just didn't want him to see us."

"Who's 'he'?"

Olbeck looked grim. "Stelios Costa."

"*No*," breathed Kate. "What was he doing?"

"Coming out of your Home Angels office building with a box file."

"No," said Kate again. "The Costa brothers are involved with a *cleaning* company?"

Olbeck pressed the accelerator and the car began to move forward. "If the Costa brothers are involved, it's quite possibly *not* a cleaning company."

They drove back to the office in silence. Kate knew what Olbeck was thinking. The Costa brothers, Stelios and Yannis, were local crime lords. Kate had rubbed up against them in her first case in Abbeyford, the kidnapping of Charlie Fullman and the murder of his nanny. She hadn't relished the experience.

"What do we do now?" she asked as the police station came into view.

Olbeck was indicating to turn into the car park. "I'm going to ask Anderton if we can put a tail on Stelios Costa. We must be able to scrape up something from the budget for that."

Kate nodded. Olbeck parked the car and they made their way back to the office. Kate's head was aching. She felt breathless, as if she was missing something important. So many different things to do and she wasn't sure where to even start. The sudden appearance of Stelios Costa in connection with the Home Angels office was a complication that she hadn't anticipated. Was it possible that Home Angels was actually a legitimate firm? In some ways it must be, given that it had supplied what seemed like a *bona fide* cleaner to the Arlens, and possibly to Adrian Fellowes. Kate thought back to Adrian Fellowes' house; dusty and musty, and uncared for. Surely he hadn't had a cleaner? Why, then, would he have had that business card? Had he been thinking of employing someone?

By this time, Kate had seated herself at her desk. Theo looked up from a pile of cardboard folders.

"Forensics are in," he said, handing her a couple of the folders. "Take a look at this. Fingerprints found at the Fellowes house match the ones found in the Arlens' bedroom, the ones we couldn't pin down."

"Arlen seemed to think it was from their cleaner, Rosa," said Kate, flipping through the report inside the folder. "I was just thinking that perhaps Adrian Fellows was employing her too, seeing as we found the Home Angels business card at his house."

"Yeah," said Theo. "That's a possibility. But seeing as we haven't even managed to track this woman down, it could be completely wrong."

"I guess you've run it through in case it's on file?"

Theo rolled his eyes. "Uh, yeah – don't you think that's the first thing I did? There's no match.

211

But—" he paused, theatrically, "there *is* a match for a second set of prints found at Fellowes' house."

Kate put the folder down. "Yes?"

Theo got up and came round to her desk, propping himself against the side of it. "Yes. A set of female prints all over the living room." He reached across to his desk and yanked over a piece of paper, which he handed to Kate. She looked at it, at the police mug shot of a young, dark woman, scowling at the camera.

"Maria Todesco," she read from the sheet. "Convictions for soliciting, drug offences..." She looked up at Theo. "So Fellowes was using a prostitute? Is that right?" She looked back down at the rap sheet and thought for a rapid moment. "Hang on. What's this got to do with Trixie Arlen? *Has* it got anything to do with Trixie Arlen?"

"I think it has," said Theo. "Forensics found two sets of women's prints all over the living room of Fellowes' house. One of them belongs to Maria Todesco. The other belongs to the unknown woman whose prints we found in Trixie Arlen's bedroom, who we believe to be Rosa the cleaner. Right?"

Kate nodded. "Right."

Theo leaned forward a little. "What if Rosa the cleaner is supplementing her cleaning income with side-work as a prostitute, a prostitute who robs her punters?"

Kate put her head on one side, considering.

"Well, I suppose it's a possibility." She looked once more at the surly face of the young woman on the sheet of paper she held in her hand. "I guess the first thing we can do is track down Maria Todesco and see what she can tell us."

Theo pushed himself upright. "Exactly."

Kate got up too. She felt that welcome pulse of excitement, an almost electrical impulse, as things slowly began to fall into place. "Let's re-interview Jack Harker as well – you know, the guy who reported a similar robbery to Adrian Fellowes – see if he recognises Maria as one of the women who robbed him."

They immediately went to Maria Todesco's last known address, a half-way house for women who had recently been released from prison. It was two streets over from the house where the bodies of the two young men who'd overdosed had been found. Kate said as much to Theo as he parked the car.

"Could be a coincidence," Theo said, "but it might not be. Mind you, this is a shit-hole of an area. You've got prostitutes, druggies and dealers all about."

"Yes, I know," said Kate. She put her hands to her head for a moment, rubbing her temples. "What if there is a connection, though? What if every single case we've had in the past month is connected?"

Theo stared at her. "How?"

"I don't know," Kate said frustratedly. "Every

213

time I think I'm getting a handle on it, it slips away again."

"Well, let's just see if we can find Maria to start with," Theo said. He knocked at the shabby front door of number fourteen, Pleasant View Drive. Kate, looking up and down the street, thought it was spectacularly badly named.

The door was eventually opened by a fat, stoned-looking girl, with long greasy hair. Her sleepy eyes widened in alarm as Kate and Theo showed their warrant cards.

"It's all right," said Theo, "We're just looking for Maria Todesco. Does she still live here?"

"Who?" asked the girl, which told Kate all she needed to know. Theo persisted, showing the girl the photograph of Maria's face.

"Oh, her," said the girl. "They, like, threw her out of here. She's a junkie."

"Do you know where she is now?"

"Nah."

"How long ago did she leave?" asked Kate.

The girl shrugged one massive shoulder. "Dunno. Weeks ago."

"Have you heard of someone called Rosa?"

"Rosa? Nah."

She could tell them nothing else. Baulked, Theo and Kate returned to the car.

"Where could she be?" Kate asked, almost rhetorically.

Theo turned the key in the ignition. "She's a prostitute and a junkie. She could be dead. She could be in prison."

"Junkie..." Kate said the word slowly, staring unseeing through the windscreen.

Theo glanced over at her. "What?"

"Trixie Arlen – you said she was a junkie too, remember? When we were doing the search?"

"Yeah," said Theo. "So what?"

Kate raised one forefinger. "Rosa was an employee of Trixie Arlen. She's also an associate of Maria Todesco, who is apparently a heroin addict."

"Right," said Theo, frowning.

Kate raised her other forefinger and entwined it with her already raised digit. "So, what if Rosa is supplying Trixie and Maria with heroin?"

Theo changed gears with an impatient shove. "So this Rosa is a cleaner, a prostitute *and* a smack dealer? Busy lady."

Kate brushed off his flippant tone. "Don't you think it's possible?"

Theo half shrugged. "I guess so."

Kate opened her mouth to say more and then realised she didn't know exactly what she was going to say. She muttered "We just have to *find* her."

"Yeah, but how? The agency's a dead-end, she doesn't have a record. We don't even know her surname."

"I don't know," said Kate, hearing her own

annoyance mirrored in Theo's snappish tone. "Has Anderton done the press conference yet?"

"I think that's going out this afternoon."

Kate tapped her lip with her finger, thinking. "Could we put out an appeal? Anyone with any information on these women contact us in strictest confidence, that sort of thing? Put Maria's details up and say we're anxious to speak to anyone who might know an associate of hers called Rosa?"

In answer, Theo pulled over to the side of the road, pulled on the handbrake and handed Kate his mobile phone. She looked at him, startled.

"It's worth a try," Theo said, simply.

After Kate had spoken to Anderton, they drove to Jack Harker's house. He apparently worked from home as a graphic designer, and his affinity with colour and visual art was clear from the moment Kate and Theo walked through the door of his small terraced cottage. The walls were painted in dark dramatic colours, the floorboards a glossy dark grey, and pictures and photographs were carefully framed and displayed on the walls like an art gallery. It wasn't exactly a welcoming house, but it certainly had style.

Jack Harker received them with his usual aplomb and another lascivious glance at Kate. She could feel Theo bristle on her behalf and wanted to laugh. Coming from him, affront at another man's lustful eyes was pretty rich.

They showed Jack Harker Maria's photograph and asked him whether she was one of the women he believed had drugged and robbed him.

He looked at it for a long moment. "I think so," was all he said, eventually.

"You *think* so?" Theo asked, and Kate saw Jack Harker frown at his aggressive tone.

"It was a while ago now," Harker said in a similarly prickly voice. "I was pretty drunk at the time. Not to mention the roofie they slipped me."

Hastily, before Theo could say anything else, Kate assured him that they were anxious to catch these women. "Anything you *can* remember could help us, Mr. Harker."

"Yeah, I know that. Thing is, I can't remember much at all. They were young, sort of pretty. Eastern European. They both had long dark hair. That really is about all I can remember."

"Did you do any drugs with them when they were here?" Kate asked.

Harker looked uneasy. "Um..."

"We're not going to press any drugs charges—" Kate began and heard Theo mutter *yet* under his breath. She fought the urge to kick him. "Seriously, we've got more important things to worry about than whether you had a joint or a few lines that night. Did you?"

Harker still looked uneasy, but after a moment, he nodded. "Yeah."

"What was it exactly?" Kate persisted.

"Um... both of those. Bit of weed, bit of coke."

"Nothing more? Nothing stronger?"

"Stronger?" Harker looked positively alarmed.

"Heroin," said Theo brusquely. "Do any heroin with them?"

Harker's eyes bulged. "Heroin? Are you kidding? No way. I've never touched that in my life."

"Hmm." Theo looked unconvinced but Kate believed Harker. She shot Theo a repressive look and turned to the other man.

"Thanks very much, sir. If there's anything else you can tell us, be sure to get in touch won't you?"

"WHAT A *WANKER*," SAID THEO explosively, as soon as Harker's front door closed behind them.

"Shhhhh!" Kate flapped a hand at him. They got into the car and Theo started the engine. Kate smiled mischievously. "You're just jealous."

"*Jealous*? Of that prick? I don't think so."

"He's clearly the swordsman that you want to be," said Kate, laughing inwardly. God, it felt good to be able to laugh at something again, even if it wasn't really that funny.

Theo snorted. "Yeah, right. He wishes."

Kate bit down on a giggle. "Anyway," she said, sobering up. "We have a tentative identification of Maria Todesco. Hopefully the press conference might bring in some more info."

As it happened, they arrived back in the office to find Olbeck and Jane watching the tail end of Anderton's address to the media on the office television. Kate felt the familiar pulse of longing at the sight of Anderton's face on screen and stamped it down. That's it, she told herself. I am no longer allowing myself to feel anything towards him. The second I get a hint of it I'm going to – to pinch myself hard. And she did just that while the others had their attention turned towards the screen.

Olbeck turned off the television and swung round just in time to catch Kate wincing. "You all right?"

"I'm fine," said Kate impatiently. "Is Anderton going to debrief us?"

"Yep. He'll be here any minute."

As usual, they heard the human whirlwind that was Anderton approach the room a minute before he crashed through the door. "Hello, everyone. Let's get started, shall we?"

Everyone settled themselves in their usual spots. Anderton began pacing the floor. "Now, I presume you've just seen my ugly mug on the telly." Kate pinched her hand again. "We've put out a request for information about the two women we believe are involved in the robbery and death of Adrian Fellowes – Maria Todesco and Rosa with the unknown surname. We've also now informed the media and the public that there is a batch of contaminated heroin out there that is highly dangerous. Hopefully that might prevent any more overdose deaths but we can't take that for granted."

Olbeck raised a hand. "I guess we've pulled in all the dealers we think might be involved?"

Anderton nodded. "Yep. Nothing from that as yet but you never know. Now, one thing you might not be aware of is the possibility that the Costa brothers may be involved. Well, I'll clarify that. Stelios Costa could be involved – apparently his revolting brother is currently overseas at the moment, Spain to be exact. I've got a tail on Stelios at the moment and he'll report back in a couple of days. Right, what else?"

It was Kate's turn to raise a hand. "Sir, we believe there's a link between Trixie Arlen's death and the death of Adrian Fellows. Rosa's fingerprints were found at both scenes. We know she was the Arlens' cleaner and possibly also for Adrian Fellowes, but it sounds more likely that she was at Fellowes' place as an associate of Maria Todesco."

"Right," said Anderton, pausing by an empty desk and lifting himself onto it to sit, swinging his legs. "You know what I think?" Everyone waited. "I think it's highly possible that Rosa might be the dealer who supplied Trixie with her gear. She may very well be the person who took all the drug evidence from the crime scene."

"So she's knowingly supplying people with

deadly drugs?" Theo asked and pursed his lips in a soundless whistle. "No wonder we can't find her. She's on the run."

Anderton shook his head. "We can't know that for certain. But it's imperative that we *do* find her."

Kate had been thinking. She raised her hand again and spoke. "There's one thing I can't work out. Why would you deal drugs which have been contaminated with this deadly substance? I thought the whole point of dealing was to keep your customers hooked so they come back to buy more and more. What's the point of giving them something that's just going to kill them? You're just going to eventually do yourself out of a customer base."

"Exactly," Anderton said, giving her a smile. She couldn't pinch her hand in his full view but she felt like doing so. "That's what doesn't make sense."

"Perhaps – if Rosa is a dealer – she doesn't know her heroin is contaminated," Olbeck suggested. "Why would she?"

Anderton nodded. "Well, almost everything we're talking about is pure speculation. What we need is some evidence. Does anyone else have anything to add?"

Nobody did. Anderton gave them a quick rundown on the findings from the Fellowes post mortem, reminded them to read through the multitude of forensic reports, and brought the meeting to a close.

Kate went back to her desk feeling dissatisfied. It was as Anderton had said – where was the evidence? All they seemed to be doing was scratching around in the dark, scrabbling for clues and coming up with nothing. She began to flip through the pile of reports on her desk but was interrupted by the telephone.

It was Kirsten Telling. She'd rung to tell Kate that the blood samples from the other overdose cases from the last month had now been tested.

"And?" asked Kate, feeling her heart rate speed up a little.

"It's as we suspected," said Doctor Telling's quiet voice. "The samples taken from Peter Hardew, Wayne Potter and John Henry Miller all show high levels of Sulatenil."

It was as Kate had feared. "Right. I understand." She thought for a moment. "Can I suggest you talk to Sergeant Bill Osbourne to see if he has anything else that might need testing as well?"

"Very well. I'll do that."

After she'd put the phone down, Kate told Theo what she'd just learned. He raised his eyebrows. "Just as well we put that appeal out," he said.

"I know." Kate got up and went over to Olbeck's office to pass on the news.

Chapter Twenty One

KATE GOT HOME AT TEN o'clock that night. Exhausted, she made a half-hearted effort to eat something before abandoning her plate of partially eaten toast. She was so tired she decided not to have her usual before-bed shower and was just stripping off her clothes by her bedside, thinking how inviting the bed looked when her phone rang.

Kate cursed and considered ignoring it, but saw Olbeck's name winking from the screen. She cursed again and pressed the 'receive' button in a resigned manner.

"You in bed?" was his opening remark.

"I wish. What's the problem?" Kate could hear the tension in Olbeck's voice and her tiredness began to abate as adrenaline kicked into her system. "What is it?"

"The station just rang me," said Olbeck. "There's a girl in reception who says her name's Rosa Ilenko."

Kate sat down on the side of the bed, winded.

"You think it's her? The one we've been looking for?"

"Yes, I do. I'm heading there now."

"Me too," said Kate, quickly. "I'll meet you there in fifteen minutes."

Driving to the station, Kate found herself picturing this mysterious Rosa. Was she a heartless drug dealer? A killer of men? Why had she handed herself in? Kate saw her in her mind's eye: long dark hair, a lean, hungry face. Vampiric. A succubus. A monster.

Yet, when Kate got to the station and made her way to the interview room where Rosa had been taken, she realised she'd been wrong. Here was only a sick and terrified girl.

Rosa was as thin as Kate had expected – thinner, even. Her blotched, grey skin was stretched tight over blueish bones that could be seen beneath their inadequate covering. Rosa was shaking and sweating, her eyes ringed with shadow.

Kate and Olbeck took one look at her and then at each other.

"Doctor," was all that Olbeck said, and Kate nodded and hurried off to make the call.

As was usually the case, the medical attendant for the station seemed to take ages to arrive. Once she did, Kate and Olbeck stood outside the room, shifting from foot to foot and waiting impatiently for the verdict.

Eventually the doctor stepped outside.

"Well?" asked Kate.

Doctor Scofield looked from Kate to Olbeck. "Well, as I expect you've guessed, she's going through quite serious withdrawal at the moment."

"Withdrawal from heroin?"

"Yes. I've given her some methadone which should make her more comfortable. That'll kick in soon and she should calm down a bit. I can leave some anti-nausea medication for her as well."

"Can she be questioned?"

Doctor Scofield nodded. "You'll have to take it easy with her. Keep her warm, make sure she's getting plenty of fluids, some food if she'll take it."

They conferred a few moments longer and then the doctor left. Kate turned to Olbeck.

"Should we proceed?"

"Yes," said Olbeck. He added, a little callously, "It might be useful. Soften her up a bit."

"Come on," said Kate. She opened the door a crack and looked through at the shivering, crying girl perched on the edge of her chair, hugging her arms across her body. "She's in bits anyway."

"We'll go easy on her," said Olbeck. "Come on."

They took her a cup of tea and a blanket. Rosa looked up at them as they entered the room. Tears trickled down her grimy face.

"Here," said Kate, handing her the warm paper cup. "Make sure you drink this."

Rosa reached out a shaking hand for it. She took a sip and then promptly retched, dropping the tea. Warm liquid splashed over Kate's legs, but she barely noticed as she helped Rosa to the wastepaper basket in the corner of the room and held back her greasy hair as she vomited.

Eventually, Rosa straightened up, shuddering.

Kate rubbed her back. "Are you okay now?"

Rosa nodded. "I'm sorry," she gasped, rubbing her mouth.

"Don't worry about it," said Kate. "Now, do you think you're going to be sick again?"

Rosa shook her head. Kate took the blanket that Olbeck was holding out and wrapped it around the girl's sticklike arms, pockmarked with needle tracks. She moved the wastepaper basket to the corridor outside.

"We need to ask you some questions, Rosa," said Olbeck. "Do you think you're up to that?"

The girl nodded, her head hanging forward. "Yes," she said, with a tremor in her voice. "I must talk, I must tell you. I need to talk."

"We'll get the duty solicitor to sit in with you," said Kate, knowing there was no point even asking Rosa whether she had a lawyer. Rosa said nothing, but nodded jerkily.

Once they were all seated in the interview room, Rosa appeared to become a little calmer. She pushed her lank hair back from her face and took a deep breath. "I came here because I was afraid. I'm afraid they will kill me."

"Who will kill you, Rosa?" asked Kate.

Rosa wiped sweat from her forehead with shaking fingers. "The men I work for. They are gangsters. They have girls working for them in a house in Arbuthon Green."

Kate glanced at Olbeck. "When you say 'working for them', how do you mean?"

"As brothel."

Kate nodded. Rosa wiped her face again. "Can you give us the names of these men?"

"One is called John, one is Terry."

"Do you know a man called Stelios Costa?"

Rosa flinched. "Yes. He is boss of the others."

Olbeck leaned forward. "Have these men specifically threatened you?"

Rosa looked frightened. Kate shot Olbeck a look and he leaned back again. Kate used as warm and sympathetic a tone as she could as she continued. "Don't be frightened, Rosa. You can tell us everything. We can help you."

Rosa clasped her shaking hands on the table in front of her. "Can you – please can you get me some gear?"

Kate bit her lip. "No. I'm sorry but no. We can't do that." She hesitated and added "Rosa, if you really want to get off heroin, we can help you with that. We can arrange for you to have treatment, to go to a clinic, anything you might need to help you. But you have to tell us everything you can before we can do that."

Rosa nodded, wincing again. "I am heroin addict. That's how they get me to do everything they made me do. I do it all for the heroin." She began to cry. "My family – my family must not know how I am. They would be ashamed of me. I was not like this back in Romania."

"Is that where you're from?" asked Kate.

Rosa nodded, brushing the tears from her face. "I come here two years ago, to study. But I run out of money and I get in with bad people and all this bad things happen."

"Can you tell us where Maria Todesco is?" Kate asked.

Rosa's pale face became even whiter. Her features seemed to shrink a little. "I think she is dead."

"You think?"

Rosa nodded. "John and Terry took her away. They were angry because of what happened at the man's house."

"What man?"

"I don't know his name. Maria and me go to his house, have sex with him, tie him up. But then he dies and we don't know how to help him. We were very scared. I called Terry and he said to leave him."

Kate found a photograph of Adrian Fellowes in one of the files on her lap. "Is it this man, Rosa?"

Rosa looked and nodded jerkily. "We didn't hurt him. We didn't hurt any of them. They wanted to be tied up, you know, it was like a game to them."

"How did you meet them, Rosa?"

Rosa wiped sweat from her face again. Kate thought that she probably should be offering her some water or tea, but remembering what had happened last time Rosa had had a sip of tea, perhaps that wouldn't be such a good idea. At least the girl wasn't shivering so much.

"The first one came to brothel," said Rosa in a low voice. "He liked to be tied up there as well. When he was paying, John spoke to him and I think he told him that we could come to his house next time. So next time, we go to his house but before we go, John tells us we have to steal all we can once man is tied up."

Kate and Olbeck exchanged glances. "You didn't argue with him?"

"With John?" Rosa's incredulous tone said it all. "Never, never argue with John. You don't understand – Maria, me, we have to do what he tells us. When he tells us. He is the one who gets us gear, you see? And if we argue with him, he beats us. So – we don't argue."

Kate understood. It was funny how she and the rest of the police had been thinking of these two girls as the villains of the piece, when it was obvious that they were as much victims as the men they'd targeted.

"How many times did this happen?" asked Olbeck gently.

"I think three – maybe four times," Rosa said. She rubbed her temples, closing her eyes as if she were in pain. Kate asked her if she had a headache.

Rosa nodded. "Such a pain in my head. My body needs drugs. How can I go without them tonight?" She looked at both of the officers with sudden panic. "I cannot do it, I cannot, you have to help me—"

"All right, Rosa, all right," Kate tried to make her tone as soothing as possible. "We'll have the doctor come and see you again tonight, after we've spoken to you. Okay? She might be able to give you a sedative, or something to help you sleep."

Rosa, having held herself rigid as she pleaded, nodded and slumped back against her chair. Kate waited for the duty solicitor to say something but the grey-haired, portly man was staring at his client with something like disapproval. Kate was conscious of a spurt of anger. Who was he to judge?

"So, let's recap," she said, as nicely as possible. "You freely admit to meeting these three, possibly four, men, tying them up and then taking their possessions." The duty solicitor shifted in his seat but Kate hurried on before he could interrupt. "Did you drug them to make sure they were nice and compliant? I mean—" She substituted another word "Did you give them drugs to make sure they wouldn't fight back?"

Rosa shook her head. "I thought we would have to. But all of them, they wanted to be tied up. For them it was sexy game, fun to do, you know?"

Kate nodded, thinking. Hadn't Jack Harker said he thought his drink had been spiked? But it seemed just as possible that he'd drunk so much he'd passed out.

Olbeck cleared his throat. "What can you tell us about Trixie Arlen, Rosa?"

Rosa's twitching body stilled. She swiped a hand under her nose, her eyes downcast.

"Rosa?" Olbeck prompted.

Rosa looked up. There was a moment's silence. Then she began to speak. "In Romania, when I am little, I want to be a veterinary surgeon. I love animals. I think I will study very hard. If you could have told me then, what I am now, I would not have believed you."

Neither of the officers spoke. Kate, regarding Rosa's thin, haunted face, imagined her as a little girl: dark glossy curls, mischievous eyes, dainty little arms and legs. The contrast to what she could see now was horrible. Pity wrenched at her throat.

Rosa was still speaking. "I come to England three – no, four – years ago. I get work as cleaner, real cleaner, I mean, not cleaner like I am for Home

Angels. But I lose my job as they don't want me anymore. When I have no money at all, I become sex worker." Her voice faded out for a moment. "By that time, I am doing heroin. It makes me feel better. Soon, I am doing anything so I can keep taking heroin."

She stopped speaking. After a moment, Olbeck asked her the question he'd asked before. "Can you tell us anything about Trixie Arlen, Rosa?"

Rosa rubbed a tear from the corner of her eye. "Home Angels send me to Trixie's house. I clean for her many weeks, no problems. And then one day, she asks me if I can get her heroin."

"Sorry?" asked Kate. "Trixie Arlen asked you to get her some heroin? Just like that?"

Rosa looked at her, sullenly. "She saw that I am addict. She knows I am. She knows that I have heroin."

Kate and Olbeck exchanged a glance. "She knew from looking at you that you were taking heroin?" Kate asked, to be absolutely sure. Looking at Rosa, she could see how that might have happened.

Rosa nodded. "She sees my eyes, so little, and the marks on my arms, and she knows. She told me her husband was the same."

"When was this?" asked Olbeck.

Rosa shrugged. "I don't know exact time. Maybe six months ago."

"So you got her some heroin?" Kate reiterated.

"Yes. She pay good money. We took it together, that first time."

Of all the things that Rosa had so far said, this shocked Kate the most. The idea of Trixie, the beautiful, famous, wealthy celebrity, injecting heroin with her poor, drug-addicted prostitute cleaner, was both incongruous and sad. That was the reality of addiction, Kate supposed: it made bedfellows of the most unlikely people.

"Did you take drugs with Trixie often?" she asked.

Rosa nodded. "Many times. I would come round at night with the gear and we would do it then. The children were always asleep."

Kate risked a look at Olbeck and saw without surprise that his mouth was crimped with disapproval. She hoped he wouldn't say anything. He didn't.

Kate pressed on. "What about the night Trixie died, Rosa?" She expected the solicitor to intervene at this point but he didn't. Perhaps he considered that Rosa had already gone too far in her confession for his intervention to make any difference at all.

Rosa shut her eyes momentarily. Then she shook her thin shoulders, squaring them as if for an ordeal.

"Trixie text me that afternoon. I go to Terry to get the gear and he give me the bag. I get taxi to Trixie's house like always."

"Wasn't that expensive?" asked Kate. "It's miles from Abbeyford."

Rosa gave her a look that indicated scorn. "She pay for it. Always Trixie pay for it."

Of course. Kate acknowledged this with a raise of her eyebrows and nodded for Rosa to continue.

Rosa dropped her gaze to the table and her thin, shaking fingers clasped together. "When I get there, Trixie is mad. Really mad. She had a big fight with her husband and he shake her. The night before that one, they had a big fight and she is still really mad."

The bruising on Trixie's arm. Kate recalled the post mortem results and realised that at least one part of the mystery was cleared up. Had Anderton and Olbeck ever taxed Jacob Arlen on that bruising? Not that it mattered now, anyway. She turned her attention back to what Rosa was saying.

"Trixie always shoots up first." Rosa gave a one-shoulder shrug. "She have the money so she go first. She had the syringe ready—" she held up her hand, clasping an imaginary syringe. "She looks at me and says 'fuck him if he thinks I'm giving this up for him'." Rosa fell silent for a moment. Again, she brushed a tear from the corner of her eye. "Then she puts it in her arm."

The interview room stilled. Kate could hear the three sets of breathing aside from her own.

"What happened then?" she asked softly.

234

Rosa's face contorted. "She died. Maybe one minute later. She fell on the bed and died."

"You knew she was dead straight away?" checked Olbeck.

Rosa nodded jerkily. "Her face – her mouth – it was blue. She didn't breathe." She took a deep shuddering breath, as if to remind herself that she herself was still alive. "I was so scared. I – I knew I had to leave her. I got all the drugs and things and I wiped around the bed with a cloth. All that time, I was doing this—" She held her hands out and shook them up and down. "I was scared more than ever before. I left."

There was another short moment of silence.

Then Olbeck asked "You left her dead on her bed and you knew her children were in the house?"

Rosa's face twisted again. She nodded and then burst into tears. "I'm sorry," she gasped. "I'm so sorry for it all. I will pay. I know I will pay. I am ready to pay."

Olbeck nodded. He looked across at Kate, who returned his nod. "I think we'll leave it there for now," he said and named the time and date before switching off the recorder.

BACK IN THE OFFICE, KATE and Olbeck faced each other across his desk.

"Blimey," said Olbeck.

"Exactly," said Kate. She leant back in her chair and rubbed her eyes. "What the hell do we do now?"

Olbeck leapt up and began pacing around the room, just like Anderton. "We have a confession. We'll have to go through with it."

"I know that," said Kate. "It's just—"

"I know," Olbeck said. "I feel sorry for her too. But she's a criminal, Kate. She might be vulnerable and exploited and fighting addiction, but she's a criminal."

"Yes," said Kate. She leant forward and put her head on Olbeck's desk, feeling depressed. "Do you think she'll get any treatment in prison?"

"I don't know," said Olbeck sombrely. "I'd like to think so."

"She'll probably get worse," said Kate. "You know what the drug situation is like in prison."

"Well, what do you want me to do?" Olbeck almost shouted. "She'll be testifying against some hardened criminals if I get my way. Believe me, heroin or not, she'll be safer in remand."

Kate sat up. "We're going after Stelios Costa then?"

"Are you kidding? The chance to put him away for trafficking – of drugs and quite possibly people as well?" Olbeck grinned tiredly. "Just hold me back."

Kate also smiled reluctantly. "Well, if you put it like that..."

"Come on," Olbeck said. "Let's run it past Anderton. Then we can go home, get some sleep, and go in all guns blazing tomorrow. Possibly quite literally."

Chapter Twenty Two

KATE WAS WAITING ON THE doorstep at five am the next morning. It was pitch black; the sky glittered with stars and the full moon was crossed and re-crossed by wispy black clouds hurrying across the sky. Kate stamped her feet to keep the blood moving, her breath steaming in front of her. Beneath her coat, she felt the reassuring bulk of her anti-stab vest. It was so long since she'd worn one that she'd forgotten the weight of it.

The lights of Olbeck's car appeared at the end of her road and the anxiety and excitement inside her leapt up another notch. She hurried down the garden path and virtually jumped into the passenger seat.

"You're keen," said Olbeck, grinning. "Here, I got you a coffee."

Kate eagerly grasped the warm paper cup with her cold fingers. "Thanks. So, are we raiding first?"

"You bet."

"Shame," said Kate. "I could just do with hauling

Stelios Costa's arse out of bed and bundling him out of the house in his boxers."

Olbeck laughed. "Well, Anderton and Theo have that pleasure. You can sit in on the interview later if you like and give him evil looks across the desk."

"I don't want to sit in," said Kate. "You know what he'll be like. He'll just 'no comment' himself to death."

"True." Olbeck hunched forward a little in his seat, peering through the dark windscreen. "It should be up here, I think."

They parked some way down from the house they'd come to enter. As Olbeck switched off the engine, Kate could see the others had already arrived: a team of uniformed officers, their colleague, Jane, wrapped in a voluminous puffa jacket, her face still smeared with sleep. There were two women there that Kate didn't recognise, both smartly dressed in black suits. No press, thank God; too early for them. Kate climbed out of the car and shut the door quietly, shivering as the cold enveloped her.

"Morning," Jane said, yawning. Several red curls could be seen peeking out from beneath her woolly hat, in jaunty contrast to her pale skin. "We're just about to go in."

Kate could see several of the officers readying the device that would force the door open. Kate had used one several times when she was on the beat and felt a flash of envy for a moment. Detective work was all very well, but sometimes all a girl wanted to do was bash down doors...

The two women came over and shook hands. The older one introduced herself as Karen Elliot and her companion as Sarah Grange. They were attending at Anderton's request, seconded from the civil service.

"We work for the Modern Slavery helpline," Karen Elliot explained, shivering a little in the cold. "DCI Anderton thought we might be able to assist."

Kate nodded. "We don't know for certain that any of these women are actually trafficked," she said. "It seems that at least a couple of them were able to freely come and go as they pleased."

Karen Elliot frowned. "Not all slaves are kept chained up, Detective Sergeant. Psychologically, whilst they might physically be able to leave their place of work, they're unable to actually go far because they've been so brainwashed."

Kate was getting impatient. "I realise that, Ms. Elliot. Perhaps we could talk about specifics in more detail after the raid?"

"Yes. Yes, of course. I'm sorry."

The woman's penitent tone made Kate feel bad. She was only trying to help, after all. Kate hastened to reassure her.

"Okay, we're off," Olbeck said, gesturing at them both to be quiet. The three women fell silent. In the quietness that followed, Kate heard rather than saw the crash of the battering ram, followed immediately by the splintering of wood and the shouts of the officers who crowded through the door.

Kate and Olbeck waited tensely. This was always the worst time. What were the officers going to find behind the door? A bunch of terrified women or a furious man wielding a weapon? Kate found herself clenching her fists and made herself relax her hands.

They waited one, two, three agonised minutes, straining their ears. Then Olbeck glanced at Kate. "Okay. Let's go. Ladies—" he nodded at the government workers, "please stay here until we let you know it's safe for you to join us."

The three officers hurried to the front door of the house, which was now hanging by one hinge. A splinter of wood from the shattered lock scraped against Kate's coat as she crossed the threshold. The house was cold and it stank: of blocked toilets, of unwashed human flesh, of rotting food. Trying not to grimace, Kate followed Olbeck through the hallway. All the overhead lights had been switched on but as they were red and purple light bulbs, visibility was poor. Red light bulbs in a brothel... Kate shook her head at the cliché.

There were shouts in the room ahead of them and a crash. Kate and Olbeck froze and then jumped back against the corridor wall as a gaggle of four burly uniforms appeared in the doorway ahead, carrying a struggling, handcuffed man between them. He was bowled along past them and out the front door, no doubt to be slung into one of the vans that were parked out of the front.

"A punter?" asked Kate quietly.

"Not this early in the morning, surely?" replied Olbeck. "We'll ID him back at the station."

They cautiously walked further into the building. The room which had disgorged the struggling man was obviously a kind of sitting room, last decorated sometime in the early eighties from the looks of the swirly-pattern carpet, pockmarked all over with cigarette burns. A filthy sofa stood against one wall and on it were four women, huddled together and shivering. There were two more women slumped against it on the floor. All were thin and shaking and terrified. Several female officers were already attempting to talk to them, offering blankets and soothing words.

Kate and Olbeck wordlessly surveyed the room for a moment. Kate wondered whether she should be talking to the women as well, to see if they could tell her anything more than Rosa already had. She even took a step forward before changing her mind. These poor girls were in no fit state to be questioned as yet.

"Come on," said Olbeck. "We need to find the drugs."

It was a struggle to get the gloves over cold fingers. Kate could feel the tip of her nose going numb as she and Jane followed Olbeck out of the room. What must it have been like for these women here, being raped and abused, spending their days naked and shivering? No wonder they turned to drugs – or, as was more likely, were deliberately given them to ensure their compliance. What kind of man would voluntarily want to actually have sex with these emaciated, strung-out, blank-eyed girls? A bad one, Kate told herself as she turned to follow Jane into another small room. A bad man. One who saw women as commodities, nothing more than that – a product to be exploited and then tossed aside when they had finished.

As it turned out, the heroin was easy to find. Upstairs, in a filthy bathroom, Olbeck pulled away the side of the bath to reveal two black rucksacks, each containing several pounds of brownish powder, some already divided up into individual plastic bags. Olbeck looked up from his search at Kate and Jane. "Not the brightest tools in the bunch, are they? Talk about a crap hiding place."

"They probably thought they were being really original," said Jane. "Stupid bastards."

"There might be more," said Kate, crouching down. She hefted one of the bigger bags in her hand. "Do you think this is the Sulatenil stuff?"

"No idea. I won't be injecting it to find out. We'll have to wait for the test results," said Olbeck.

Kate grinned. She heaved herself to her feet. "Are you going to tell Anderton?"

Olbeck got up, groaning a little. "God, my back. Yes, let's get back to the station while SOCO get to work here. Anderton's going to be a very happy man."

"Let's see Stelios Costa 'no comment' his way out of this one," Kate said vindictively, as they made their way back to the car.

WHEN THEY ARRIVED BACK AT the station, Olbeck sprinted off to the interview room where Anderton was enclosed with Stelios Costa. Kate decided to check on Rosa. As she peered into the holding cell through the peep-hole, she braced herself. But Rosa was sitting up in bed quite calmly and quietly, clasping her hands over her knees.

Relieved, Kate pushed open the door. "You're looking better, Rosa," she said, sitting down at the other end of the narrow bed.

Rosa didn't exactly smile but her face relaxed a little. "I feel better. I feel as if I was in a dark cloud and now it is starting to break, a little."

"That's good to hear," said Kate. "I'm glad because I need you to come with me for a moment. There's something you can do for me."

Immediately, Rosa tensed. "What?"

"Nothing bad," soothed Kate. "We've arrested several people who were present at the building that you indicated was a brothel. You remember you gave us the address?"

Rosa nodded cautiously. "You have arrested them? For Maria's death?"

A little taken aback, Kate shook her head. "Not specifically for that, no. We're still gathering evidence. What I need you to do is identify the two men that we currently have in custody. Can you do that for me?"

Rosa's sense of calmness was rapidly disappearing. "What if they see me? They will hurt me, I know it."

Kate hastened to reassure her. It was only after several minutes of persuasion that Kate was able to get the girl to go up to the interview room floor with her and an accompanying officer, where the man who'd been arrested at the brothel was currently under surveillance in the room with a one-way mirror on the wall.

"Here, Rosa," said Kate, gently positioning the girl so she could see into the room. "Can you identify this man?"

Rosa gazed through the glass, her thin, grubby fingers at her mouth.

"Is Terry," she said eventually.

Kate nodded. "Thank you." She left Rosa in the care of the PC who'd accompanied them up to the viewing room and quickly ran to the interview room where Anderton and Theo were. She knocked.

"Detective Sergeant Redman has entered the room," said Anderton. All four men in the room looked at her: Anderton and Theo inquisitively, Stelios Costa and his lawyer with a frown. Kate murmured her request in Anderton's ear and although he looked surprised, he nodded.

"Two minutes, Kate," was all he said. Happy with that, Kate straightened up and left the room, shutting the door firmly behind her. Hopefully her little intervention would at least have given Stelios Costa a few minutes' worry if nothing else came of it.

Back in the viewing room with Rosa, Kate watched Terry being removed by several officers. The door of the room shut and then opened again and Stelios Costa was ushered in. Anderton and Theo remained by the door.

She saw Anderton's mouth move as he gave an instruction and Stelios turned to face the mirror. Kate saw him smile as he looked straight ahead and was momentarily disconcerted. It was as if he could actually see them.

She could feel Rosa begin to tremble beside her. "It's okay," she said. "Don't worry, he can't see you. Can you identify this man, Rosa?"

Rosa was breathing fast. After a moment, she said in a voice so small, it was barely audible, "It is Costa, his name is Stelios Costa."

"Thank you," said Kate. A positive identification

at least. Now they just had to make sure that Rosa would testify as a prosecution witness, and then finally they might be able to jail one Costa brother for good.

"He is such a bad man," said Rosa, still in an almost whisper. "I always think his face is like a shark."

Kate looked at Stelios, looking at them. She knew what Rosa meant – it was something in his eyes; a blankness, a void, nothing behind the flat black gaze.

"He can't hurt you here," she said, anxious to reassure Rosa. "You're perfectly safe."

Rosa stood still, hugging her thin arms across her body. "I know he does bad things but I never see him angry," she said. Then she looked up at Kate. "Only when the bald man comes once. That was the only time."

"Sorry?" asked Kate. "What bald man?"

Rosa shrugged, turning back to look at Stelios again, who was being ushered out of the door by Theo. "I don't know. He came one, two times. Last time Stelios was very mad." She relaxed a little as the viewing room door shut. "I am very tired now."

"I'll take you back to your cell," said Kate, nodding at the PC. They walked slowly back down the corridor, Rosa and the PC in front of Kate, who was puzzling over what Rosa had just told her. Was it significant?

It wasn't until they reached the cell floor that things began to fall into place. As Kate realised the significance of what she'd just been told, she stopped dead, as if she'd just walked into a heavy, immovable object. Surely – was she wrong? She *had* to be wrong – but what if she wasn't?

"Take Rosa into her cell," she asked the PC. "I'll be back in a minute."

Kate sprinted back up the stairs to the office floor, wondering what the quickest way of obtaining the photograph she needed would be. After a moment of hesitation, she went over to the paper recycling box by the window and dug through it. Would it still be here? Just as she was asking herself the question, she spotted it and pulled out the crumpled paper with a cry of triumph. Then she wheeled around and ran back down the stairs again.

"Can you let me in?" Kate asked the PC, who was just turning to go. He looked surprised but nodded, reaching for his keys.

Rosa had sat back down on the edge of the bed and was biting her nails. She looked up in surprise as Kate came in.

Kate held out the paper with its front page photograph. "Is this the bald man you saw with Stelios Costa?" she asked, puffing slightly.

Rosa looked at the spotted, creased paper for a long time, frowning slightly. Then she nodded, a quick bob of her dark head.

"You're sure?" persisted Kate.

"Yes, it was him."

"Good girl." Kate turned to go, anxious not to delay even for a moment. Then, at the cell door, she turned round. "Rosa, for what it's worth, I think you're an extremely brave person. You really are."

Rosa finally smiled, a little wanly. Kate smiled back in response and then she was out the door and across the floor to the stairs, running as fast as her tired legs would carry her.

Olbeck was back in his office, thank God. Kate almost fell through the doorway, still clutching her paper. He looked up, surprised. "What's up?"

"I'll tell you in the car," said Kate. "We need to go. I'll drive."

Chapter Twenty Three

THEY APPROACHED THE HOUSE JUST as the sun was starting to set. The reddish light blazed off the autumn colours of the trees as they drove slowly down the winding driveway, gradually descending into the hollow of the valley. The beautiful, lonely house was before them. It had a blank, closed-in look, as if nobody lived there.

Kate parked the car and they rang the doorbell. Kate was expecting the small, dark-haired housekeeper to answer the door, but nobody came. She looked at Olbeck, raising her eyebrows.

"Try again," he said. "This house is so massive, it might take ages to get to the door."

Kate rang the bell again and knocked for good measure. There was no answer. "Well..." she said, stepping back a little. "Do we force it?"

As she spoke, Olbeck tried the door handle. It moved easily in his grasp. "It's open."

They stepped into the house, announcing their presence in muted shouts. Kate expected to see either the housekeeper or Michael Dekker himself appear, alarmed at their sudden entrance, but again, nobody came. The house felt empty. Their footsteps sounded inordinately loud as they crossed the marble floor of the hallway and passed into the rooms beyond.

Kate walked towards the orangery at the back of the house, merely to ascertain that it was empty. But seated in the same chair as he'd been sat in when she'd visited before was Michael Dekker. For one frozen moment, she thought he was dead – he was so silent and still, staring out at the view beyond the window with glassy eyes. She and Olbeck stopped and she almost jumped when Dekker spoke.

"Come in, Detective Sergeant. Do sit down."

Kate and Olbeck remained standing, watching Dekker, who hadn't taken his gaze from the window. He looked diminished; smaller, somehow, than he had at their last meeting. There were grey shadows beneath his pale blue eyes. His hands were folded together in his lap and his legs were tucked under a tartan blanket.

"Won't you sit down, officers?"

"Do you know why we're here, sir?" asked Olbeck.

At last Dekker moved his gaze to look at them. He smiled a little. "I saw on the news you'd arrested Stelios Costa. I guessed it wouldn't be long before you paid me a visit."

"We need you to accompany us to the station, Mr. Dekker."

Dekker smiled again. "Would you mind if we spoke here, just for now?" He looked at them directly again. "I'll tell you everything again later, at the station. I've got nothing to hold back now. But if we could talk here...?"

Olbeck hesitated. Then he nodded. "Very well, Mr. Dekker." Kate and he moved further into the room as he spoke the words of the caution. Dekker said nothing for a moment, but Kate saw him close his eyes briefly as the charge of murder was mentioned. Then he opened them again and an air of calm resignation touched his features.

Kate and Olbeck seated themselves in the two armchairs that faced Michael Dekker's seat. He continued to look past them, staring into the distance. Once they had settled themselves, he turned his gaze back to their faces.

"Do you wish to have legal representation?" asked Kate. Something about his stillness, his aura of fatalism, was making her faintly uneasy, without her being able to put a finger on exactly what it was.

Dekker shook his head. "Not just now. Perhaps later."

"What did you want to tell us, Mr. Dekker?" asked Olbeck.

"Everything," said Dekker, simply. "Everything. I'll start by telling you about my health. About a year ago, I was diagnosed with an inoperable, incurable cancer." He tapped the side of his bald head. "Up here. The doctor told me that I had only months to live."

"I'm sorry to hear that," Olbeck said, frowning a little.

"It's probably why I decided to finally act," said Dekker. Then he shook his head, as if dislodging the thought. "No, no it's not. I know why I decided." He shifted a little in his chair, unclasping his hands. "I saw Trixie Arlen earlier this year. I think I told you so before. I almost bumped into her, but as it happens, she didn't see me. It was the same day as the anniversary of David's death. I couldn't have had a clearer sign than that."

"A sign to do what?" asked Kate gently.

Dekker looked at her in surprise. "To kill her, of course. To kill her. I should have done it years ago."

"You admit to killing Trixie Arlen," Olbeck said. "Is that right? Why?"

Dekker looked at him as though he were stupid. "Do you have children, Detective Inspector?"

Olbeck shifted a little in his seat. "Not yet."

Don't ask me, prayed Kate. But Dekker's attention, for the moment, was entirely on her partner.

"I think if you had children you might understand. Trixie Arlen was not the golden girl, the nation's sweetheart that she liked to be seen as. She was a monster."

Dekker's gaze had somehow narrowed and

sharpened. Despite his illness, for a moment, he pulsated with real energy. It was hate, Kate realised. Strong enough to kill.

Seeing that the detectives weren't going to say anything, Dekker continued. "Trixie Arlen killed my boy. She murdered him as surely as if she plunged a knife into his heart. She killed her first husband too, and the baby that she lost. All of them."

For the first time, Kate began to doubt his sanity. She looked anxiously over at Olbeck but he was staring at Dekker steadily.

Dekker carried on speaking. "I can see you don't believe me. Trixie's own mythology was quite seamless. Of course, she told everyone that her first husband, Ivo Wright, was the one with the drug problem. Would you believe me if I told you that it was Trixie who introduced *him* to drugs? Within a year of meeting her, he was a hopeless drug addict. She did the same to David."

Kate didn't want to interrupt him but she couldn't quite let that go. "Don't you believe that people make their own choices, Mr. Dekker? Didn't your son decide to take heroin of his own free will?"

Dekker look at her, smiling gently. "Addicts don't have free will, Detective Sergeant. The first time David took heroin was the start of his addiction. He didn't realise it then, of course. Trixie lied to him, as she lied to everyone else. She lied to the entire country about who she was."

This time, Kate didn't speak. She realised that further interruptions would be futile. This man had a story he wanted to tell, probably a story that he'd wanted to tell for a long time. All she and Olbeck had to do was listen.

"Everyone was so sorry for her," Dekker was saying. His mouth twisted a little. "The poor young widow who then lost her baby. You know *why* she lost the baby? She was still taking drugs, of course. She cared so little about the life of her unborn child that she continued to take drugs during the pregnancy and then, of course, the baby died."

"How do you know this, Mr. Dekker?" Kate hadn't wanted to interrupt but she couldn't help herself.

"David," said Dekker, simply. "David told me everything the night before he died. After he told me, he went home and injected himself with an enormous quantity of heroin. I think he wanted to die. His life, by then, was such a source of misery to him that I think he didn't want to carry on."

There was a moment's silence. Dekker raised one trembling hand to his eyes and brushed away what could have been a tear.

He started to speak again. "I don't know why I didn't kill her the second I realised what she was. When David died I was – I was so – I couldn't function. I could barely live, let alone plan. So... so time went on and Trixie still lived, and I went on doing what I did, but I never forgot, you see.

255

You never forget. They say time heals everything but that is nothing but a lie, I'm afraid. You never forget. Every morning on waking – every morning – I have a couple of seconds of pure happiness, did you know that, Detective? Just a few seconds before I remember, and then it's like reliving the day he died, over and over again."

Dekker's voice had grown hoarse. He stopped speaking for a moment, clearing his throat, before he began again. "When I saw Trixie that day, I knew I had to act. At first I thought of killing her myself. I wanted to do it. I wanted to see the fear on her face. But when I began to think about it, I realised I could do society more than one service. I could remove Trixie Arlen from the face of this Earth and in doing so, get rid of as many drug addicts as I could at the same time. Let Trixie kill herself as I knew she would one day. There was as certain poetic justice in it that appealed to me."

Again, he stopped speaking. After a moment, Olbeck leaned forward. "It was you who organised for a shipment of heroin to be contaminated with Sulatenil?"

Dekker nodded. When he spoke, he sounded almost proud. "When you're rich, Detective Inspector, you can do pretty much anything. You can arrange for chemists and manufacturing laboratories and whatever ingredients that you need. All you need is money. Did you know that?"

"No," said Olbeck. "I wouldn't know."

"Well," said Dekker. "Now you do."

Outside, the sun had almost set. Shadows were creeping across the marble-tiled floor of the conservatory, entwining Dekker's blanketed feet in darkness. Kate could see the blood-red clouds on the horizon as the last of the daylight began to slip away.

Dekker was still speaking. "I went to Stelios because I knew he was exactly the kind of man who would do as I asked. He was surprised, of course. I think he thought when I first made the appointment that I wanted to do something with his legitimate business interests." Dekker chuckled. "He soon came round to the idea, though. He could see the profit in it. And no doubt he also thought it would also make excellent blackmail material if it ever came to that."

"Did he realise that you'd contaminated the heroin with Sulatenil?"

Dekker looked surprised. "Of course not. Where would be the profit in that for him? No, Stelios thought he was distributing heroin in the 'normal' way. I knew he would be able to ensure that Trixie Arlen was given the drugs that would kill her, without realising what he was doing." He was quiet for a moment. "Of course, when people began dying, he realised something was wrong. But by that time, I'd achieved what I set out to do. I didn't care much about the rest of it anymore." He paused again and then said, "I don't care anymore. I can't really bring myself to care that much about anything."

Olbeck and Kate glanced at each other. They waited for Dekker to go on speaking but it seemed that he'd come to the end of his confession. The silence stretched on and on, as the room gradually darkened.

Eventually Olbeck stood up. "Mr. Dekker, you'll have to accompany us to the station now."

Smiling again, Dekker shook his head. "I don't think so."

"It's not a request, sir."

Dekker was still smiling. "I won't be going anywhere."

"You—"Olbeck began, but that was all he had time to say. Dekker's hand slipped down to the blanket on his lap. It delved beneath the tartan fabric and came up swiftly, holding something. For a frozen moment, Kate thought it was a gun and she was on her feet before she realised it was a syringe. Before she could say or do anything, Dekker had plunged the needle into his thigh, stabbing himself through the blanket, and depressed the plunger.

Rosa had said it had taken Trixie Arlen a minute to die. Michael Dekker didn't even have that long. In the twenty seconds it took Kate and Olbeck to reach him, to pull the syringe from his leg, a spurt of blood coming with it, he was dead. He sagged against the back of the sofa, his head rolling to one side.

Olbeck dropped the syringe and it fell to the hard floor, rolling away beneath the sofa. Kate stood trembling, looking down at Dekker's blue-tinged mouth and half-open eyes.

"Oh God," was all that Olbeck said, in a low, aghast tone. Kate said nothing but she groped for his hand as the last of the sunlight finally slipped below the horizon.

Chapter Twenty Four

"Wow, you look like shit," was Theo's heartening remark as Kate flopped into her chair the next morning.

"Gee, thanks. Hardly surprising is it?" countered Kate. She put her handbag under the desk, noticing a brown envelope on her desk as she straightened up. Frowning, she got up to make herself and Theo a coffee.

"Thanks," said Theo, as she handed over a brimming cup. "You know we charged Stelios Costa with everything we could throw at him?"

"I heard," said Kate. "Fantastic. Let's just hope we make it through to the trial."

"Well, yeah." The two of them were silent for a moment, remembering the other times they thought they'd had the Costa brothers firmly in their sights only for them to slip away under the instruction of their highly paid and ruthless legal representation. Theo brightened a little. "Still, fairly watertight case, this time round. Particularly if it really is true that Maria Todesco is dead."

Kate yawned. "Do we have any evidence of that? They might have just moved her to another brothel."

"Let's hope so," said Theo. "Let's really hope so."

There was a short silence. Kate looked at the pile of reports that needed attention, squared her shoulders and pulled the first one towards her.

"So, did Dekker really just kill himself right before your eyes?" Theo asked suddenly, leaning over the desk.

Kate flinched. "Can we not talk about it right this second, thanks?"

"But did he?"

"Yes. And there will probably be hell to pay. That's why I don't want to talk about it. Okay?"

Theo said nothing. Instead, he sauntered round to Kate's side of the desk and gave her cheek a hearty smacking kiss. She reared back in amazement. "What the hell are you doing?"

"You'll be all right," Theo said, grinning. "You'll be just fine."

He wandered off, whistling a little tune. Kate looked after him with raised eyebrows. Then, shaking her head and smiling despite herself, she turned back to her desk.

She sipped her coffee and picked up the brown envelope, turning it over in her fingers. She had a nasty feeling she knew what was inside it. In an act of cowardice unlike her, she opened her desk drawer and dropped the envelope inside it, shutting it up out of sight.

The day passed slowly in a blur of paperwork, phone calls and many cups of coffee. Towards the end of the day, Kate found her gaze being drawn back to the closed desk drawer. She tried to ignore it, turning her attention to the final report that she'd planned for the day. Once that was signed and complete Kate sat back, tapping her pen against her jaw. Leave it for today, she told herself. Wait until you're not quite so knackered and burned out. She switched off her computer and stretched, easing the ache in her neck. Then, in a rush, she pulled open the drawer, yanked out the brown envelope and quickly slit the back of it with a trembling finger.

She read the first line *we regret to inform you that in your recent examinations for the position of Detective Inspector...* and slumped back in her chair, closing her eyes. Bitter regret surged up her throat. If she'd just worked harder, studied harder, spent more time actually focusing on passing the exam... Kate leant forward, pressing her fingers into her eye sockets, dangerously near to tears. What an *idiot*. She'd applied for the exams in such confidence – *I'll breeze through them* – and to realise that she had, in fact, failed was a bitter pill to swallow.

She soberly folded the letter back into its envelope, not wanting to read it here in the office, and put it away in her handbag. Looking up, she realised she was alone in the office – just as well, as she felt as if she were about to burst into tears at any moment – but at the same time, she felt a sharp surge of loneliness. Slowly, she got up, pulling on her coat.

As she turned to leave, Kate's gaze fell on the neat pile of reports she'd completed during the day. She remembered Rosa, so scared but so determined to do what was right. She thought about all the women who'd been in that stinking house, and what their lives must have been like. Really, when you thought of it like that, what did a silly exam really matter? You're good at your job, Kate, she told herself. You can retake them. In the grand scheme of things, it *really doesn't matter*.

Feeling a little more cheered, she marched out of the station and stopped on the top steps. There, standing side by side, with their hands in their pockets were Olbeck and Jeff. They looked up at her and smiled a greeting.

"Were you waiting for me?" Kate asked, feeling a burst of happiness at the thought.

"Who else?" said Olbeck. He extended his arm as Kate came down the steps and she took it, hooking her other arm under Jeff's. "We thought we'd go for tea and cake. We need to talk *weddings*."

"Oh God," said Kate. "That sounds ominous."

"You're our best woman, darling," said Jeff as they began to walk down the street. "You can't get out of it now."

Kate squeezed his arm. "I know, I'm joking. I'm thrilled." They walked a few more steps while she wondered whether to say anything and decided that yes, she would. What were best friends for, if not to listen to your troubles? "I failed my exams."

"Oh bugger," Jeff said, just as Olbeck said over the top of him.

"That's a shame but don't worry about it, just retake them. You'll ace them next time."

"Yes," said Kate stoutly. "I'm sure I will."

Their six feet shuffled through a rustling pile of autumn leaves. The daylight was fading and a chill wind made them all huddle into one another as they walked. Kate could feel the warmth of Olbeck and Jeff on either side of her and she sighed with deep thankfulness that despite everything else, she still had her friends. That was all you needed, really, wasn't it? When you got right down to it. That was all that really mattered.

They turned the corner of the street and Kate could see the welcoming lights of the tearoom up ahead.

"Come on," she said, "I'm buying. It's the least I can do."

"Nice one," said Olbeck and they walked up the steps of the tearoom together.

THE END

Enjoyed this book? An honest review left at Amazon, Goodreads, Shelfari and LibraryThing is always welcome and *really* important for indie authors. The more reviews an independently published book has, the easier it is to market it and find new readers.

Sign up to Celina Grace's newsletter here at her website http://www.celinagrace.com for news of new releases, promotions and other goodies. You can unsubscribe at any time and won't be bombarded with emails, promise!

More books by Celina Grace...

Hushabye (A Kate Redman Mystery: Book 1)

ON THE FIRST DAY OF her new job in the West Country, Detective Sergeant Kate Redman finds herself investigating the kidnapping of Charlie Fullman, the newborn son of a wealthy entrepreneur and his trophy wife. It seems a straightforward case... but as Kate and her fellow officer Mark Olbeck delve deeper, they uncover murky secrets and multiple motives for the crime.

Kate finds the case bringing up painful memories of her own past secrets. As she confronts the truth about herself, her increasing emotional instability threatens both her hard-won career success and the possibility that they will ever find Charlie Fullman alive...

Hushabye is the book that introduces Detective Sergeant Kate Redman. It's available as a free ebook download on Amazon, iBooks, Google Play, Kobo and Nook, and as a paperback from Amazon.

Requiem (A Kate Redman Mystery: Book 2)

THE GIRL'S BODY LAY ON the riverbank, her arms outflung. Her blonde hair lay in matted clumps, shockingly pale against the muddy bank. Her face was like a porcelain sculpture that had been broken and glued back together: grey cracks were visible under the white sheen of her dead skin. Her lips were so blue they could have been traced in ink...

When the body of troubled teenager Elodie Duncan is pulled from the river in Abbeyford, the case is at first assumed to be a straightforward suicide. Detective Sergeant Kate Redman is shocked to discover that she'd met the victim the night before her death, introduced by Kate's younger brother Jay. As the case develops, it becomes clear that Elodie was murdered. A talented young musician, Elodie had been keeping some strange company and was hiding her own dark secrets.

As the list of suspects begin to grow, so do the questions. What is the significance of the painting Elodie modelled for? Who is the man who was seen with her on the night of her death? Is there any connection with another student's death at the exclusive musical college that Elodie attended?

As Kate and her partner Detective Sergeant Mark Olbeck attempt to unravel the mystery, the dark undercurrents of the case threaten those whom Kate holds most dear...

Requiem (A Kate Redman Mystery: Book 2) is the second in the Kate Redman Mystery series. Available from Amazon now.

Imago (A Kate Redman Mystery: Book 3)

"THEY DON'T FEAR ME, QUITE the opposite. It makes it twice as fun... I know the next time will be soon, I've learnt to recognise the signs. I think I even know who it will be. She's oblivious of course, just as she should be. All the time, I watch and wait and she has no idea, none at all. And why would she? I'm disguised as myself, the very best disguise there is."

A known prostitute is found stabbed to death in a shabby corner of Abbeyford. Detective Sergeant Kate Redman and her partner Detective Sergeant Olbeck take on the case, expecting to have it wrapped up in a matter of days. Kate finds herself distracted by her growing attraction to her boss, Detective Chief Inspector Anderton – until another woman's body is found, with the same knife wounds. And then another one after that, in a matter of days.

Forced to confront the horrifying realisation that a serial killer may be preying on the vulnerable women of Abbeyford, Kate, Olbeck and the team find themselves in a race against time to unmask a terrifying murderer, who just might be hiding in plain sight...

Buy Imago on Amazon, available now.

Snarl (A Kate Redman Mystery: Book 4)

A RESEARCH LABORATORY OPENS ON THE outskirts of Abbeyford, bringing with it new people, jobs, prosperity and publicity to the area – as well as a mob of protestors and animal rights activists. The team at Abbeyford police station take this new level of civil disorder in their stride – until a fatal car bombing of one of the laboratory's head scientists means more drastic measures must be taken...

Detective Sergeant Kate Redman is struggling to come to terms with being back at work after long period of absence on sick leave; not to mention the fact that her erstwhile partner Olbeck has now been promoted above her. The stakes get even higher as a multiple murder scene is uncovered and a violent activist is implicated in the crime. Kate and the team must put their lives on the line to expose the murderer and untangle the snarl of accusations, suspicions and motives.

Snarl is the fourth Kate Redman Mystery from crime writer Celina Grace, author of Hushabye, Requiem and Imago. Available now from Amazon.

FURTHER INFORMATION

talktofrank.com
http://www.talktofrank.com
For information on drug use, drug addiction,
legalities, treatment and advice (UK site).

Beyond the Streets
http://www.beyondsupport.org.uk
A UK based charity working for women involved
in prostitution. They run a free, confidential
support helpline for women working in
the sex industry – Tel: 0800 133 7870

Modern Slavery
http://www.modernslavery.co.uk
A UK government-funded body which
advises and assists in identifying and
stopping modern day slavery. They run
a free helpline – Tel: 0800 0121 700*

EXTRA SPECIAL THANKS ARE DUE TO MY WONDERFUL ADVANCE READERS TEAM...

THESE ARE MY 'SUPER READERS' who are kind enough to beta read my books, point out my more ridiculous mistakes, spot any typos that have slipped past my editor and best of all, write honest reviews in exchange for advance copies of my work. Many many thanks to you all, with special mention to Donna Woltz, Margaret Hill, Kathleen Charon, June Donnelly, Margaret Gardiner, Shannon Watz, Patricia Steele, Beth Bruik, Erin DePino, Rene Ellis, Mary-Ann Courtenaye, Wanda Sue, Anne Dannerolle, Andrea T, Cathlin Barry, Melissa.

If you fancy being an Advance Reader, just drop me a line at celina@celinagrace.com and I'll add you to the list. It's completely free, and you can unsubscribe at any time.

ACKNOWLEDGEMENTS

Many thanks to all the following splendid souls:

CHRIS HOWARD FOR THE BRILLIANT cover designs; Andrea Harding for editing and proofreading; Kathy McConnell for extra proofreading and beta reading; lifelong Schlockers and friends David Hall, Ben Robinson and Alberto Lopez; Ross McConnell for advice on police procedural and for also being a great brother; Kathleen and Pat McConnell, Anthony Alcock, Naomi White, Mo Argyle, Lee Benjamin, Bonnie Wede, Sherry and Amali Stoute, Cheryl Lucas, Georgia Lucas-Going, Steven Lucas, Loletha Stoute and Harry Lucas, Helen Parfect, Helen Watson, Emily Way, Sandy Hall, Kristýna Vosecká, Katie D'Arcy and of course my wonderful and ever-loving Chris, Mabel, Jethro and Isaiah.

This book is for Chris Howard, my immensely talented cover designer, with very grateful thanks.

Printed in Great Britain
by Amazon